HUNTERS
OF THE
DAWN

A NOVEL

>────────<

William K. Thayer

Interior design by Booknook.biz

For our grandchildren
Finn, Ella, Micah, and Desi

TABLE OF CONTENTS

PROLOGUE

THE COLUMBIA RIVER HAS BEEN FLOWING *into the Pacific Ocean since long before human beings began to live along the ocean's coastline. One of the four largest rivers of the North American continent, it is 1,249 miles in length from its headwaters which drain out of Columbia Lake in Canada to its mouth near Astoria, Oregon. It begins in mountainous terrain, journeys through arid regions and alluvial valleys before cutting through rocky bluffs that form a great gorge, and, finally, passes through coastal forests and spills into the ocean.*

The forested regions of the Oregon coast even today are beautiful. But one can only imagine how they must have looked in prehistoric times. The massiveness and ubiquity of the old growth trees. The green lushness of the vegetation that grew in the meadows and low-lying regions of the coastal habitat. The richness and the diversity of all the wild plant and animal life, flourishing, yet unassailed by the harmful destruction of modern man with his penchant for loosing chemicals, chain saws, and bull dozers into beautiful natural ecosystems that had remained balanced and sustainable for thousands upon thousands of millennia.

Beginning ten thousand years or more ago as many as thirty different tribes of people lived in the Columbia River Basin. They were hunters and foragers who, some eight thousand years ago, became reliant upon fishing for their primary means of securing food.

The lower river tribes tended to stay year-round in small settlements centered around community and individual family huts built for permanence from wood from the coastal forests, with entryways and ventilation and light openings secured or partially covered by animal skins. Ultimately, as their sophistication with woodworking increased, these settlements became primarily multifamily plank house villages.

Further inland, in contrast, tribes would move now and again, as the harshness or temperate nature of the four seasons and food supply dictated. The dwellings of these more nomadic groups were temporary structures, made up typically of poles, mats, and skins, each structure capable of being broken down, packed up, and moved as part of the occasional migrations necessary to the upriver tribes' survival.

It must have been a fascinating and challenging epoch in the history of humankind.

This is a work of fiction. It is a story of primitive life, family, leadership, and survival focused on a lower Columbia River Basin tribe, some eight thousand years before Europeans, horses, and steel arrived in North America.

chapter one

SALMON

SALMONIDS OF ONE SORT OR ANOTHER *have graced the Columbia River ecosystem for at least ten million years, since long before mankind inhabited the North American continent. Chinook, coho, sockeye, chum, pink salmon, and steelhead trout are still with us today, although not nearly in the numbers that once flourished. Before extensive human exploitation of the fish began with the arrival of white settlers in the mid-1800s, some ten to sixteen million adult salmon and steelhead returned annually up the Columbia River to spawn.*

In olden times, before the white man came with his horses and steel, a Native American sat on a riverbank, where sand swept down into the green water, and watched.

The river swelled before him. Birds worked the surface. Less than two stones' throw away from shore, a brown-backed slick mammal rolled, a harbor porpoise, sunlight flashing off its dorsal fin, rattling spray into the air before it dove and gave chase to something below the surface. Shiny glimmerings twinkled the surface as tiny fish flitted across wave tips, seeking an escape from chrome hunters marauding below.

Yes, it was time.

He stepped into the water, squatted on his haunches, and scooped a handful of water up to his lips. Tasting it, he spat. Salty, at last.

He jogged upriver to a dugout canoe and slid it off the sand until it floated free. He leapt in just as it was leaving the shallows behind.

The spear was there, alongside the paddle. He grabbed the latter, and with graceful strokes drove the lithe dugout along the escarpment—out to where the sands disappeared and the green of the water had a turquoise tinge. With a flick of the paddle he subtly adjusted course, back shoreward, paralleling to keep the drop-off in view.

Soon, silvery shapes began to flash beneath him. He slowed his craft, half-spun it, and brought it back into the shallows—approaching a small inlet where clear freshwater tumbled into the salt from narrow cuts through an alluvial deposit at the creek's mouth.

There, baitfish had bunched, and large coho were slashing into them in a feeding frenzy. Embroiled in their own life and death struggle, the fish large and small ignored the narrow shadow of his canoe as it silently slid up over the surface of the water just above them.

He traded paddle for lance, deftly fastening a noose-bracelet of greased sinew that was fixed to the spear around his wrist, before re-gripping the spear at its balance point.

With great force and remarkable precision he thrust the spear down, into and through a great buck coho, pinning the salmon to the soft river bottom momentarily. Drawing the lance back by its cord, the fish came with it, thrashing. Blood stained the water and sprayed the hunter as he leaned down, one of his hands expertly snaking around its tail and the other coming up from the belly, behind the caudal fins, fingers digging into gill slits.

He drew the struggling fish into the boat and immediately sank his teeth into it, just behind the skull, crushing its backbone.

It went still. He cast it into the bottom of the dugout, and traded spear for paddle.

The current had shoved him upstream several hundred yards, the tidal surge still strong. He re-oriented the vessel and shot it back to the inlet.

But too late. It was over, the menagerie of prey and predator had moved up with the flood of the incoming salt water. He could see the birds working far upriver. It all happened so fast.

Well, he had enough. This fish would feed her and the little ones, and cut well for jerking the balance in the next day's hot sun.

He felt good. The taste of blood and salt in his mouth. His back and arms, strong and true, had delivered.

The light of the sun was waning. It would fade, the great orb would be replaced by the bold little white one, and then a new day would dawn. And twice, the sea would invade the river, bringing his people its riches, the fish that fed his family and all of his proud tribe.

He would be ready. His eye keen. His spearhead sharp. His body fed, rested, and strong.

He would be ready.

chapter two

AH'NECCA AND ALOUK

ER CHILDHOOD HAD NOT BEEN ESPECIALLY *unusual for a Native American girl of that early era. After the age of two, she was an only child, her older brother and younger sister having both passed when the last great sickness had come to the tribe.*

Then, when Ah'necca was but six years old, she lost her father. A hostile tribe from inland had raided the small village in which she lived with her family. Ah'necca's father and other males of her tribe had successfully driven off the invaders. But her father was wounded; struck by a spear in the gut. Infection had developed, and he had died eight days later.

His passing into the spirit world had left her mother and surviving daughter unprotected, both from enemies, and starvation. Ah'necca's mother had tried to attract a new mate, but none of the tribe's men were willing.

For a time, Ah'necca's uncle begrudgingly shared his family's food with Ah'necca and her mother, but then his woman abruptly put a stop to that, and Ah'necca and her mother began to struggle to stay fed.

Being only a few years younger than him, Ah'necca had played with Alouk when they were little. Then, after he had proven his warrior status in the skirmish that had led to Ah'necca's father's death, Alouk had suddenly taken a different interest in Ah'necca.

When the young man's overtures began, Ah'necca was not ready. She pushed him away.

But her mother saw advantages. Her mother knew she and her daughter would not survive many winters, if even one more, without a hunter to procure meat for them. She knew they were at risk of capture and subjugation to slavery by the hostiles, without a warrior ready to defend them. Alouk had become a man, and a worthy one at that. She prevailed on Ah'necca to accept him. And so she did.

They moved him into their hut.

Two winters later the first baby came along. It was a boy.

Ah'necca was instinctively a good mother. With their first child, she also had the wisdom of her own maternal parent still there to guide her.

Next spring, another child was born. It was a girl.

In those initial years, Ah'necca and her mother took turns foraging, and caring for the children.

While Alouk hunted. Fish, rabbits, squirrels, waterfowl, and occasionally, a deer or elk. He was a strong man, with good spear and club skills. He often found success in his pursuits of meat.

In the third year following her union with Alouk, Ah'necca's mother took ill. She did not recover. As she died, however, she was stoic. She patted them both on the head. She wished them well, closed her eyes below a knitted brow, and then her spirit flew to join the pelicans as they winged in formation out over the river.

It was a great loss for both of them, Alouk as well as Ah'necca. Grandmother had been such a help with the children. She had been such a reassuring presence for Ah'necca whenever Alouk was out hunting.

But she was gone now. And perhaps because of the loss of another parent, Ah'necca's subconscious was frequently calling back memories of the invading hostiles that had attacked their tribe back in her childhood. Violence and bloodshed indelibly etched in her brain; graphic visuals from the skirmish which had led to the maiming and death of her father.

He had been gone the entire day. The sun was down now. Ah'necca clutched at their youngest child and shuddered involuntarily. She tried pressing out the bad thoughts. She needed Alouk.

They had become as one, she and Alouk, some four years earlier. When she was still but an adolescent.

She had grown increasingly emotionally attached to him since they had joined, but mainly, the reality was that she and their children's survival depended heavily on him. His skills as a hunter, and his reputation and fierceness as a warrior, kept them secure.

Her day's foraging concluded, and with twilight approaching, she had brought the two little ones into the hut.

In the hut, she fed the children dried eulachon, freshly picked camas root bulbs, and a handful of salmonberries each. She did not eat herself, waiting to do so with Alouk when he returned. She had just tucked the children into their elk skin bedding and was listening to their breathing as they dropped off to sleep, when she heard the soft fall of footsteps outside the hut.

She leapt to her feet and reached for a small handheld bludgeon lying by the door to the hut. She poised, arm raised, ready to strike. As a shadow passed outside across the doorway, she heard the hiss of a whisper. Recognizing his voice, she instantly relaxed. She dropped the weapon and took Alouk into her arms as he pushed through the leather door and entered the hut.

She did not fail to notice that he smelled strongly of salmon. The hunt must have gone well. She was overwhelmed with relief and gratitude.

chapter three

TURTLE

Berries, roots, plant leaves, stems, and *flowers, and certain types of fungi, as seasonally available, made up the plant-based part of their diet; while the flesh of deer, elk, bear, rabbits, squirrels, possums, frogs, turtles, lizards, snakes and other wildlife, and birds (such as geese and ducks along with their eggs and young), as well as marine animals (including shellfish, pinnipeds, otter, and the occasional beached ceta-cean) contributed protein to their diet, when available.*

Rain drops dimpled the surface of the shallow lake. She slipped out from behind the cover of the underbrush at the shoreline on the marshy end of the lake, into the dank, still water. Her garments had been left behind—rumpled, in a heap, cached in a low-sitting nook of an ancient maple tree.

She moved very slowly. Only tiny ripples emanated from her progress as she continued to move deeper into the lake toward a small island. She had seen a large male turtle on its bank, just the day before, when she and the children were picking berries. The turtle's flesh would be a welcome change of pace from the monotony of dried fish that they had been relegated to consuming, since the end of the summer salmon runs, to satisfy their hunger for meat.

At first light she had left Alouk and the children asleep in the hut. Their daughter usually arose first, being the youngest; and Ah'necca expected that by now, the little girl had already awakened the boys.

She had made sure Alouk knew what she was doing, and had told him that he could expect her to return before dark.

Turtles were wary. She did not know how long she would have to lie—still, naked, and clean. But first, she had to get clean. The water was cold, but not unbearable. When the muck was up over her ankles, and clear water was lapping at her thighs, she lowered her body into the lake, all the way up to her shoulders. The cold enveloping her was a shock. She knew it would get worse before it got better, braced, and tilted her head back, immersing herself completely underwater. There she lingered, holding her breath until she felt about to lose willpower over her lungs.

She controlled her exhalation carefully, bubbles escaping as she moved her torso and head upright, out of the water, slowly. Her motions were almost imperceptible. She waited for the pond water to drain off without splashing from her hair, then she finished rising, ever so gently, and stood still momentarily. Trembling slightly, waiting until the water was once again completely still around her legs to resume her progress toward the island.

The island itself was tiny, not much larger than the interior of the village's community hut. Vegetation on its main body was heavy, except for its banks. A dense thicket with patches of rhododendron, salal, and wax myrtle bushes. But where the water lapped up against the nearly circular border of the island, there was sand and gravel exposed in a strip about as wide as she was tall.

Her plan was to insert herself into the dense underbrush on the island, with her body hidden—facing out to the part of the beach on which she had seen the turtle the day before, crawling up onto the island.

If her bathing had been sufficient, he would not smell her. If her trembling was not excessive, he would not see or hear her, at least until it was too late. She knew turtles could be remarkably fast when threatened. But she was confident of her own quickness. If the turtle beached itself again in the same place; she would be within leaping distance. But whether it would return, and if so when, those were the unknowns.

The uncertainty did not worry her. It was a simple matter. She would wait, and it would happen, or it would not.

She stepped softly onto the beach and worked her way as quietly as she could into the cover of the brush. It was as if she had disappeared. The lake's surface was still again, except for a multitude of tiny circles which blossomed as each drop of rain fell upon it.

Alouk woke with his daughter jumping on him. Laughing. It was already light out. He had slept longer than he usually did. Their son was still asleep. Alouk gathered his little daughter into his arms and began playfully tickling her feet. She giggled loudly. Her happiness caused the boy, her older brother, to raise his head, annoyed at her having ended his slumber.

Alouk took the children out of the hut and away from the settlement. This was a routine. The tribe wisely kept its members' excrement at a safe distance from the village, up in the woods and away from the river. When the three of them had each done their business, Alouk took them down to the riverbank. This also was a routine. There, the three of them shed their daily wear, and one at a time immersed into the sharp coolness of the river. Scrubbing briskly—hands and under the nails of their fingers first, and then their bodies all over, using grit from the gravelly river bottom.

After bathing, they dressed, filled several deerskin water carrier bags with water from the river, and shaking with cold but refreshed, they returned to the hut.

He did not know how long Ah'necca would be gone. He knew that she needed a diversion, and, if she succeeded, the turtle meat would be a delicacy for the afternoon meal.

They ate as a rule but twice a day, assuming that there was enough food for them to do so. As lower river people, they often had enough food, as the spirit of the river tended to be generous. But the animals and fish they killed for survival had been hunted and fished by many generations of humans before. They were crafty and making a kill was always a challenge. Even if plentiful, at times the tribe members' efforts to capture prey failed. And the plants, seeds, roots, and berries that made up the balance of the tribe's diet would occasionally fall into short supply because of over-harvesting. It was a drawback of living permanently at just one site.

Alouk pondered the alternative. The hostiles, in contrast, were nomadic. When their food supply at a particular site became scarce, they would just pick up and move. As they traveled, they would evaluate the scarcity or abundance of game and edible plants in passing through any region. They would keep moving, or stop and settle, whichever, as the evident availability of food suggested was most prudent. He knew this about the hostiles because Elish'tie, another member of his tribe, had lived with a band of them at one point. She had been captured as a girl, and then kept as a slave for several years before managing to somehow escape. She would not, however, share with anyone in the tribe much detail about her experiences over the time of her absence. Other than that her escape, and the fact that she found her way back to her birth tribe, had been orchestrated by the spirit of íkuli, the whale.

Once back in the hut, Alouk fed the children. The acorn harvest the preceding fall had been good. There weren't many oak trees in the lowlands, but there were enough within a few days' walking distance to help support his tribe. They had learned to get to where the oak trees grew more abundantly early in the fall, before squirrels and birds had hidden or destroyed the oak grove's bounty of acorns. Their harvest, thankfully, had been good that year. He and Ah'necca, along with other tribal members, had been able to gather, roast in large clam shells on hot coals, crack open, and grind the nut meat of a great many acorns. The acorn flour their hard work had produced had been stored in thick baked clay jars, protected by heavy, snug-fitting lids.

He scooped a small handful of the flour from one of the clay jars and mixed it with water from one of the deerskin water bags they had filled that morning, working on a flat raised bench with a hewn wooden surface that the family used solely for food preparation. He added several handfuls of salal berries from an unsealed earthen pot. He and the children ate the mush, scooping it with their fingers, until the meager servings he had prepared were gone.

The rain that morning had been light, and Alouk had allowed the boy and girl to join several other tribal children on a small hillside within sight of the hut, where it appeared they had created and were enjoying a mudslide.

He himself had returned to his labors from the night before, tanning an elk hide.

He had been absorbed with that task, other than one eye on the children as they were laughing and playing with their friends in the mud, when she became visible.

He could, even from a distance, see that she had killed the turtle. Carrying it in a sling on her back—its tail sticking out from behind the bun of her hair and an ear—as she approached.

Having closed the distance between them, she stopped before him, even as he rose to greet her. He saw the trace of a smile flit across her lips, and a light of joy briefly flicker in her eyes. She was so beautiful to him. Especially in this moment.

The turtle was enormous for its kind. It occurred to him that it must have been a leader of its clan. He mouthed a word of gratitude to its spirit, thanking its family and clan for their sacrifice to the benefit of his own family and tribe.

This fine turtle's carcass would feed several families, or, if joined with other families' catches of the day and made into a stew, possibly the whole tribe.

He embraced Ah'necca briefly, and then nodded appreciatively as she passed to go into the hut. His eyes followed her as she disappeared behind the hanging entryway cover.

She was amazing.

He would keep the children outside and occupied, unless the rainfall became too heavy, and let Ah'necca sleep.

She had earned it.

chapter four

ELK

Т HE LAST GREAT ICE AGE, WHICH GEOLOGISTS *place at having occurred between ten and twenty thousand years ago, resulted in sheets of ice across the North American continent, shortly after the emergence of the Bering Strait land bridge which some anthropologists surmise led to the beginning of a human population in North America.*

The large prehistoric beasts of the Paleolithic era that had roamed North America during the ice age—the woolly mammoth, giant ground sloth, dire wolf, cave bear, North American camel, and saber tooth tiger—died off as the great sheets of ice melted away. The oceans swelling again to their present levels as the water runoff from the dissipating ice returned to its original home.

In the first century which followed the year 6,000 B.C., when the tribe of Alouk and Ah'necca lived, the geography, climate conditions, and weather patterns of the Pacific Northwest coastal region would have been like what one would experience during any given season in that area today.

Springtime is fresh and vibrant, the beginning of the season for growth and blossoming vegetation. Frequent rain showers interrupted by days of bright, warming sunshine.

Summers, generally warm, with an ambient temperature in the range of 70 to 100 degrees, occasionally cooled by spates of low-lying shrouding fog, or rain squalls which are sometimes accompanied by thunder and lightning.

Fall, gloriously temperate. Wet at times, but not unpleasantly so. Still plenty of warm days enabling the harvest of the most substantial of the great fish runs to occur in relatively comfortable conditions.

But winter, ah winter! Doggedly cold. Snow rare, and short-lived when it visits. And so, not cold in a singularly life-threatening sort of way, but rather, just always and persistently chilly, especially because of the soaking wetness that the heavy winter rains, which may last for weeks on end, and periodic bouts of heavy shore pine-bending winds, add into the mix to complicate matters.

It was winter. The village supply of dried salmon and eulachon was dwindling. Much of the smaller game in the coastal regions where the tribe lived had migrated south, was in hibernation, or, because this was neither a mating nor food gathering season (during which they would at times be distracted and more easily captured), the animals were at their wariest. Alouk and Ah'necca's store of dried berries had been exhausted and their supply of acorn flour was low. Likewise with the other families in the village. The tribe would have to wait until spring for the fresh growth of roots, flowers, and berries before more could be collected.

It was cold out but a temporary lull in the days of drenching rain had finally occurred. The ground was soaked and the forest floor spongy as Alouk and three other men embarked on a hunt for an elk. It was understood they may be gone for more than a day. Many of the tribe's adult males remained behind within the village. Some of those would venture out on day quests for deer or small game while the elk hunting party was gone, but solo, and only in a rotation that left intact within the village something in the way of a defensive warrior presence. The village's children, their mothers, and elders must stay protected, always. The tribe's primary threat, ever of concern, was mainly invasion by a hostile inland tribe, but a watch against the possibility of risk to individual tribal members, from a particularly aggressive grizzly or black bear, cougar, or wolf pack was routinely maintained as well.

The first day the elk hunting party was out, it located a small elk herd. It would be good if they could make a kill while no more than a day out because of the reduced distance that they would have to transport the meat, bone, and hide back to the village.

Having found fresh elk sign, they crept up but were careful to not give the elk any opportunity to detect their presence. They observed the herd for a while, then Alouk and his fellow hunters retreated.

They made camp some distance away, where they found and killed a porcupine, sharing it—uncooked as they did not want the nearby elk herd to smell woodsmoke from a campfire. Skinning it out beginning at the quilless belly, they consumed all its meat, including its heart, liver, and kidneys for their day's meal, knowing it would strengthen their bodies and help prepare them for what was to come.

Then they rested and considered the next day's strategy.

Elk are large and very strong animals—at full adult maturity often weighing more than the combined weight of all four of the hunters. The antlers of a bull elk could penetrate and kill a man easily. Alouk's tribe avoided bulls. But the hooves of any cervid are a formidable weapon, also. Elk and deer can rear back and plunge forward with great force, doing much damage with front hooves, not to mention the hazard from trampling and kicks from rear hooves. It was impossible to trap and hold an adult elk in a snare, as could be done with hares, squirrels, ducks or geese. Unless perfectly placed, a spear thrown from more than an arm's length, alone, would not bring an adult elk down. The coastal terrain did not lend itself to driving an elk off a cliff or other precipice. Chasing them into a river had produced a successful kill for the tribe only once—on other occasions when it had been attempted, the elk that had taken to water had been lost to the river's current, even after having been disabled by blows and spears delivered from the hunters in dugout canoes.

Their best strategy, unfortunately, was hand to beast combat, dangerous as it was. And to make a kill by hand inevitably required engaging in close quarters at great risk, and the physical interplay of more than one strong hunter.

The plan agreed upon, they relaxed, quiet in the darkness, closing their eyes in alternating shifts over the course of the night. Two on watch, two at rest. At daybreak, they rose and left behind the beds of sword fern leaves they had lain upon.

They bathed themselves in a pooled section of a small brook that meandered nearby where they had camped. After thoroughly scrubbing themselves to reduce human scent as best they could, they quietly returned to the area where the small elk herd had been spotted the day before.

The herd was still there, in a long meadow decorated with well-grazed scrub grasses interspersed with sporadic bunches of scraggly salal. The open area was hemmed in by brush, except where it phased out on opposite ends into narrow game trails that led through copses of red alder and big leaf maple trees hovering above thick, bunched brush.

In watching them the previous day, Alouk had calculated, correctly, that the elk would likely tend to enter and leave the meadow by traversing one or the other of those two trails.

The hunting party split in half, and two of the men moved—in a flanking maneuver that kept them downwind of the elk herd and out of its sight and hearing range—to one of the trail access points. The other two hunters, remaining unobtrusive as well as they set up into position, angled around outside of the perimeter of the opening to the trailhead at the opposite end of the meadow. Once there, all four men embedded themselves in the brushy growth along the exiting trails.

Alouk waited until he was confident all were in place. He had a line of sight to several of the elk herd. He handed his spear and knife to his immediate companion, Il'mecma, and unleashed his hardwood bludgeon from the sling that he wore across his waist and over his shoulder. Il'mecma helped him strap it with sinew against one of his wrists, secured with a slip knot for quick release. He then nodded at Il'mec-ma and moved a hand up to his lips.

Cupping his fingers around his mouth, twice in rapid succession he mouthed a sharp squawking sound. The noises pierced the silence in a near perfect imitation of a blue jay's scolding call, one used by that species to warn other jays of predators nearby.

The grazing elk came to attention. Their heads swung abruptly up, and they stopped chewing grass. They had placed the sound but waited for more. Alert but slightly confused, as they could see nothing, and they could smell nothing. Alouk knew they were prepared for flight, but it was obvious too that they were uncertain of where the danger was approaching from, and thus hesitating to act until they had confidence of the direction to which they should flee.

At that moment the two hunters at the opposite end of the meadow suddenly appeared, sprinting toward the herd, spears in hand.

The elk herd bolted. Quickly getting up to speed and heading straight at Alouk and Il'mecma's position.

Alouk let the first animals pass, including the big bull who ran in the middle of the herd. His focus was a thin cow whose gait was unsteady, making her last to arrive. He had watched her closely, during their surveillance of the day before. He knew she was old, and if the spirits were willing, her time had come. She was the most vulnerable, in this herd.

Just before she came abreast of him, he rose out of the underbrush and leapt, into her, his chest colliding with her shoulder, knocking the wind out of him and no doubt creating an explosion of panic and fear in her. But Alouk's initial surge got his arms over her back and momentum carried him up to where he was essentially nearly astride her. He bore down with thigh muscles to hold on. She continued to run, smashing into the brush along the trail trying to scrape him off, but her speed was slowed by his extra weight and the imbalance it added to her flight. Able to breathe again, he dodged his head around, ducking branches, and then reached forward with one hand, grasping for an ear or one of the striding front legs, whichever first he could grab. It was difficult; but he thought of what would happen if he lost his position and fell under the flailing sharp hooves of his quarry.

Il'mecma was pursuing, running behind them, but even with the old cow encumbered, he could not outrun her. Behind Il'mecma were the other two of the hunting party, making up the distance from where they had initiated the surprise attack, anxious to join in the kill.

Alouk sensed that he was losing his position astride her. Suddenly, however, the old cow had to make a sharp turn at a bend in the trail where it steeply twisted uphill, and Alouk's reaching hand was able to catch a hold on one of her ears. He yanked back with all his might. Her head pivoted involuntarily. She tried running with her head twisted back but couldn't maintain balance. They went down, hard. He was thrown over the old cow's head shoulder first into the rocky trail, but came up in a flash, bludgeon in hand. He brought it down with all his might, even as she was leaping up, pounding it against her right front foreleg. There was a dull thud as the blow slammed into her leg, bruising flesh and smashing bone.

The old cow knocked Alouk back as she leaped up and began to limp in a haphazard run ahead along the trail, endeavoring yet to escape her pursuers. But her speed was half of what it had been. Il'mecma passed Alouk and caught up with her. He stabbed one of the two spears he was carrying into her buttock, slowing her down further. Alouk joined them and was able to dive in front of her, brandishing his club. As she wheeled to cut off trail, Il'mecma drove Alouk's lance between her first two ribs. Still, she did not fall. She reared back, flailing hooves at them as the two men pivoted around her, cutting off any path to flee in whichever direction she whirled. Soon, the other two hunters were upon her too.

They did not have to wait long. She went down, and a bludgeon ended her suffering.

The huntsmen paused. A great spirit had just passed. An elder of the mooluk, whose body would now nourish their own tribe for much of the balance of the winter. It was neither a time for sadness, nor a time for celebration. It was a time to act. They had much to do. To bleed this animal, butcher it, and transport its body parts, most of which their people had a dedicated use for, back to the village.

Il'mecma bent down to the cow's neck, grasping the butt of his bulky stone knife, and began to hack at the old cow's throat. The others waited, ready to cup their hands. One at a time they would each receive a share of its first spilled blood, in honor to the fallen prey.

chapter five

WHALE

THE OCEAN WAS BUT A SHORT *jog from the village. Members of the tribe visited the beach frequently. It was a source of food, but also of clam and mussel shells that were relied on by the tribe in a variety of different ways. The large heavier scalloped clamshells could be fractured into spearpoints or knives that were devastatingly sharp and effective for cutting into flesh. Unbroken mussel and clam half shells could be used domestically as cups, bowls, and spoon-like dipping utensils.*

Alouk had ventured to the coast one morning intending to forage live clams and crab, as a change of diet for his immediate family.

He saw the whale as he approached the beach. He could see it was an adult, and one of the larger of the cetacean species that would infrequently be cast upon the shoreline.

The tide was out, and its great black body was stranded above water in a rocky inlet that formed a small bay.

He had paused upon topping a rise, just before the terrain descended out onto the gravelly beach. As he had scanned the vista extending seaward—an innate precaution he took before ever stepping out into an open area—there it was, an íkuli. Out of water, and evidently yet undiscovered by another tribe or any other large predators.

He did not go any closer. Once he had assured himself no other persons or creatures were feeding on it, he retreated and ran back to the village.

Having received news of this unexpected bounty from Alouk, Ty'ee, the tribe's leader, organized a gathering party to return to the beach. Other than by two warriors—who were assigned as protectors of the group and thus remained armed as usual with spear, club and knife—only cutting tools, leather packs and large baskets were carried by the eight tribal members chosen to harvest the whale. The group traveled light, and soon they were looking down on the beach.

Standing at the hilltop location from where Alouk had earlier spotted the whale, they visually scouted the beach area below. The whale remained undisturbed.

One of the group's two armed warriors was left posted on the hillside, as a lookout, while the balance of the group proceeded down to the beach.

As Alouk with the others approached the whale, he did not touch it. Instead, he waited, as did the others, watching their tribal leader, Ty'ee, for permission and guidance.

The animal was enormous. Its spirit had already left it, but apparently only very recently. The still wet and glistening hide led Alouk to believe that it had, in fact, delivered itself onto the beach for them in the dimming light just before daybreak.

Ty'ee, the tribal leader, had governed the tribe ever since Alouk was a child. It was the custom and obligation according to tribal law in matters of opportunity such as this one presented—where food enough for the entire tribe might be at hand—to immediately notify the head of the tribe of the discovery, and then abide by the leader's decisions as to the harvest and distribution amongst tribal members. This was why initially none of the harvest party which was gathered around the íkuli with knives in hand stepped forward to begin. They waited for Ty'ee to speak.

From alongside the great corpse, his own height less than half the tallness of the beast's massive girth, Ty'ee meted out instructions to the recovery party. He identified the sections of the whale allotted for he and his woman, those for the families of the warriors, and on down the line. Here, though, with this harvest, there would be plenty—even of the most cherished parts of the whale—so obtaining his blessing was more of a formality than a restriction which would limit the shares received by the lesser classes of the tribe.

The harvest party fell to its duties, cutting into the whale with stone and shell knives, tearing and hacking out chunks, filling baskets and packs, and strapping loads on to each other's backs. They then began to traverse from beach to village, and back again, for more and more. They always maintained two groups, keeping one at the whale, working on it, and the other group hauling the packs and filled baskets. Each group with an unencumbered warrior ever-present and on the ready to defend.

The process continued until it was dark, and then was resumed at first light. By the end of the second day, the tribe had as much as it could possibly process, and left the remnants of the whale's carcass, which were substantial, for such other tribes or predators as might discover it before it had putrefied.

Meanwhile, in the village, multiple fires were kept slow burning throughout the day and night. With all tribal members who weren't on duty as sentinels for the tribe or directly involved with the harvest and transport hard at work in cutting up, salting, and drying strips of whale meat and blubber.

Larger chunks of whale skin that had been separated from the edible tissues were immersed in soaking vats—soft sided containers that had been created over time from seal skins and which were kept for communal tribal use regularly filled with oak chips and water—to preserve and start the tanning process. Tanned whale skin sections, when ready, could be thin sliced in a circular pattern to make long strips which, along with processed deer, elk, and bear hides, and tendons and sinews preserved and dried from all big game (all ultimately soaked in or rubbed with fish oils or animal grease), would enrich the tribe's store of string and cords.

Forage parties were sent out to carry or drag back to the village extra firewood and brush necessary to support the enhanced fire needs.

Once the recovery and transport party had finished making its trips to the beach, Alouk joined Ah'necca in the village. There they worked tirelessly alongside others processing the whale flesh. The village children, except for the very youngest, assisted. Four times the large yellow orb, followed by its smaller white cousin, graced the heavens, before the tribe was finally done with preserving and storing away the meat.

It was mid-day. Alouk was amongst the remaining workers, cleaning up at one end of the village. As he doused the last of the extra fires that had been kept hot until the meat was finally all preserved, he noted an increase in the volume of voices around him. A buzz of excitement was spreading amongst those nearby.

Ty'ee had walked to a rise in the center of the village utilized for meetings and announcements. Alouk saw this and moved to join the growing throng of villagers there. Ty'ee paused, and then raised his arms. The village fell silent.

Alouk joined his family and the others gathering about Ty'ee, watching him.

The leader initially just stood there, arms still in the air. Apparently until he was sure all his people, other than the sentinels, were present and prepared to listen.

Then, he spoke. He blessed the íkuli, and its sacrifice. He honored its great spirit by picking up and breaking a spear into four pieces, and then laying the broken shaft pieces in a circle at his feet.

Alouk knew what this demonstration signified. It meant that other big game would now be spared death indefinitely; that is, left un-hunted by the people of his tribe until Ty'ee should return and pick up the circle of the broken spear and deliver its spearhead to the village spear maker. It was understood that small game, fish and shellfish, and birds could continue to be harvested as desired to supplement the tribe's meat diet. But that all deer, bear, and elk were to be left alone until further notice. Perhaps even until the next great fish run entered the river, which Alouk knew was now not far off.

Ty'ee closed the ceremony by advising the tribe to rest. They had done well, he said, and they should focus on family time and instructing their children in the ways of the tribe, foraging, and individual life skills until the cache of whale meat became small.

While they listened to Ty'ee, Ah'necca's arm had been resting on Alouk's shoulder. As the talk had ended, she lowered it and took the hand of their son. Alouk put his arm around their daughter as he reached for Ah'necca's free hand. Together, in a state of peaceful exhaustion, the four of them walked from the village meeting to their hut.

The work done for now, it was time to sleep.

chapter six

COUGAR

SHE HAD INADVERTENTLY NAMED HIM.

As Alouk handed the bloody—but still somehow beauti-ful—howling little bundle of newborn boy over, it had occurred to her. He was a gift from the spirits.

Her eyes raised to meet those of her man as a smile of real-ization lit her face; she had arrived at motherhood. Exhausted but gratified, she said softly, "po'la".

What had started as a mere knot in her abdominal region was now a precious being, small but full of vigorous life. In-stinctively calming once placed in her arms and against her skin.

She rested the child's face by her one of her swollen breasts, wincing only once, briefly, as the baby began suckling. Ah'nec-ca then promptly fell asleep.

From then on, her abbreviation of the tribe's native word for "gift", "Po'la", became what they called the boy.

↣

He was small and wiry in appearance, which belied his re-markable strength and quickness. As a child of only five win-ters now, he could outrun, out climb, out swim, and even occasionally outsmart many of the older kids and adults in the village.

But as is often the case with precocious youngsters, he also had a powerful streak of independence. He tended to think and act ahead of his age and was beyond anxious to grow up and prove himself as a warrior. His father was proud of Po'la's exuberance and prowess for a mere child, and earlier, during the wet season, had fashioned for Po'la a handsome and sturdy stone knife. Thereafter, the boy carried it with him ceaselessly, not infrequently putting it to good use, contributing a variety of small animals, lizards, and snakes to the family's diet.

On this day, all were enjoying the warmth of a welcome interlude of springtime sunshine.

His parents Alouk and Ah'necca, together with Po'la's little sister, were ahead, near the tail end of a group as it was making its way back to the village after a day's foraging. They were passing along the flank of the tallest peak standing within a day's travel from the village. Il'mecma led the way, while another warrior by the name of Tilkeshi, at that moment keeping the company of the fair maiden Elish'tie, brought up the rear.

As they descended along the elk trail, the boy Po'la perceived a jerky movement off to one side, just a flicker of motion before it disappeared. A squirrel. The little rodent had, as it endeavored to create a space of safety from the human entourage that was passing through its homeland, imprudently rounded behind the trunk of a massive fallen western red cedar tree, but without keeping the boy and the group of humans within its own line of sight.

Po'la knew it had given him an unexpected advantage in having taken its eyes off of him before arriving at a point of safety. He ducked off trail, darting quickly and noiselessly around to the side of the deadfall at which he knew the squirrel would likely reappear. He would have one opportunity. He was excited.

He would have been right—and a nice treat of western gray squirrel meat would have been on the menu for the family's late afternoon meal—but for one thing, which the squirrel saw in time but unfortunately Po'la did not.

An adult female cougar was crouched on a low-extending branch of a grand maple tree. Her greyish white belly hidden by the branch on which she was resting, her tawny brownish-beige coat and the black markings around tail, ears, and nose blended seamlessly into the shadowing from the canopy of conifers rising above the trail. She was not more than a stone's throw from the trail.

The very tip of her long tail had twitched just once, no doubt as she pondered the line of people passing close by and evaluated her chance of turning one of them into a meal for herself. But the squirrel had seen the subtle movement of the tip of the big cat's tail, and suddenly reversed its own course, darting down under the old fallen cedar trunk instead of circumventing it as Po'la had assumed would happen. Deeming the preoccupied humans it had been concerned about before the lesser of the risks than the pensive cat that was now on its radar.

Rounding the end of the cedar trunk and finding no squirrel in sight, Po'la was surprised, and inquisitive. He knew it was near; he had not seen it leap to any nearby standing tree limb, and he was sure it wouldn't have turned back toward or gone across the trail given that there were others on the trail that had been coming up behind Po'la. The boy crouched down, correctly surmising the little creature had escaped by darting under the fallen trunk. He peered into the crevasses below the bark of the trunk, assessing whether any might have allowed the squirrel an escape route, or if possibly it might be still trapped, right there, where he could easily kill it with the stone knife he had in his hand.

Meanwhile the big cat in the maple tree had seen its opportunity. She had been reluctant to attack the group. But the boy was close, distracted, and of perfect size and vulnerability for a quick kill. In just moments she could be done and retreating into the forest, with a meal firmly in her jaws.

She dropped from the tree limb and moved toward the boy. The soft pads of her feet landed quietly, but not silently enough. Po'la heard the sound and reacted. The cougar leaped just as the boy screamed and rolled. The cat's powerful jaws missed the back of the boy's neck by inches, but her grasping foreclaws raked across the space where he had been, just touching his moving shoulder. Po'la was able to get his feet under him enough to find purchase and dive under the huge, downed cedar tree's trunk, wedging himself against its stringy thick bark and the ground beneath, face out to meet the attacking predator, with the sharp point of his stone knife raised upward. Inaccessible on three sides, the cat would have to drag him out of the cave-like hollow into which the boy had barely managed to scuttle, to be able to get its jaws around his neck for a kill.

But his scream had startled the cat, causing it to rear back and pause momentarily. With what paltry space for flailing that he had under the constrictions of the overhanging log, the boy instinctively waved the knife out from his entrapped position. The tip of the knife pointed into the tawny beast's face, as she snarled and gathered to pounce and finish her catch.

But Po'la's initial scream had caused his parents and the rear guard of the adults that had been proceeding down the trail to realize he was not with them, and obviously in horrible danger.

Elish'tie was there first, through the brush and yowling with weapon in hand, facing the cougar, at the ready. Tilkeshi, Ah'necca and Alouk immediately behind her, spears and knives brandished, and now, too, yelling at the cat.

The cougar turned and fled, angry that she had been deprived of her meal, but sensible enough to know that the odds had flipped. This was no longer going to be a safe meal; it would be a fight against too many of these bold and angry humans and their weapons, and the cat wasn't that desperate.

Ah'necca and Elish'tie gently aided the boy out from under the downed cedar. He was shaken, but not crying. There was but a skin-deep gash, from the top of his collar bone area down to his right elbow. It looked bad at first, as blood was oozing out of it and had mixed with dirt and smeared over much of his right arm. But closer inspection reassured Ah'necca that it was not a deep wound. He would be fine.

His mother took the boy into her arms and held him tight. There would be a time to better understand how it had come to be that she and Alouk had lost sight of this precious child for any moment at all, let alone long enough for this terrifying event to have occurred. But now was not that time. She just gripped the boy and told him, over and over, that he was safe.

Her heart was filled with gratitude. This child, she and Alouk's first gift from the spirits, had been spared, on this occasion.

But the world in which they lived in was not always an easy place to survive. She would need to do better. She looked imploringly at Alouk, as he stood by with their daughter at hand, watching her holding Po'la. Deep concern written in the tight, weathered lines of his face.

She knew, even without words, that he knew.

They would need to do better.

chapter seven

⊠EER

COLUMBIAN BLACK-TAILED DEER ARE INDIGENOUS *to the Pacific Coast. With a brown coat and the top of their tail bearing the namesake black strip of hair, they stand about shoulder height to an adult person and average eighty to one hundred twenty pounds in weight at full maturity. They have excellent sight, smell, and hearing and have, since time immemorial, recognized humans as one of their top predators. An herbivore, they thrive living at the edge of the forests, browsing on grasses, leaves of poison oak, salal, and salmonberry bushes, young maple tree leaves and new growth Douglas fir and western red cedar needles, deer fern, and lichen growing on trees. They tend to feed most actively at dawn and dusk.*

Alouk had killed the buck early in the day. He carried it first to the village. Draped over his shoulders, holding its front legs in one hand and its hind legs in the other, clasped against his chest like the wings of a shawl. Striding confidently home, remnants of blood from the bleeding process dripping from the hacked throat of the deer. The buck's head, hanging upside down in front of Alouk's right thigh, swayed with the rhythm of his steps.

Upon his arrival, Ah'necca and the children gathered skin water bags and followed Alouk to the bank of the river near the village. There, in the gravel at the water's edge, Alouk lowered the buck. He bent over it and opened its belly with the sharp edge of a special knifelike tool that had been fashioned from a fractured clamshell. He removed the edible organs and the deer's stomach and intestinal tissues, the latter which would be used along with the animal's skin and most of the rest of its body parts. The balance of the offal he piled into a heap that he would later take out in his canoe and drop over its side into a deep part of the river.

Six turkey vultures circled above him as he worked. Delicately tilting and dipping in response to subtle changes and wind currents as they did so. The little human family's appearance at the river's edge had dislodged them from the tattered remnants of a rotting sturgeon carcass on which they had been feeding. Having gotten a whiff of the huge but long-dead fish, Alouk marveled at the vulture's ability to survive on putrid meat.

The children splashed in the shallows. Ah'necca began severing off the buck's head. Sawing at the neck with her knife. Once she was through the soft tissues, they would break the neck vertebrae. Then she could take the head aside and gradually work at removing the buck's brains and antlers. Getting out intact the brain matter, needed for the hide tanning process, was a difficult assignment, a deer's brains being encased deep within the tough and stubborn skull compartment. The antlers, in contrast being comparatively easy to break free by simply smashing at the base of each antler with a large rock. The tines of each would be saved for later use in making spear points and fashioning into other tools.

Gradually, the buck's remains were processed by Alouk and Ah'necca, with many chunks of beautiful venison cleaned in the river, and those and all other useful parts transported to the family's living area. The boy and the girl helped carry the loads from the riverside to the hut.

Over the next several days the buck's meat, such as they and their neighbor's had not been able to eat roasted fresh that first night, was dried, smoked and stored. And Ah'necca began the process of tanning the deer's hide, which had been soaked in cold saltwater and left in a cool corner of the hut until she was ready to work on it, into buckskin. This skin, which she intended to end up as a piece of plain leather which could be fashioned into a garment, would be prepared with all hair removed.

Ah'necca, like all her fellow villagers, had grown up trained in the old ways. How these intricate processes had been developed, by whom, and when, no one alive now knew. But these were the means of survival that were next to instinctual with the tribe. These were the processes and rituals that Alouk and Ah'necca's children were observing, absorbing, and learning fastidiously so that when they were adults, they could pass them along to the next generation.

First, Ah'necca stretched the "green" deer hide out, initially fat side up, and staked it to the ground near the hut. She diligently worked its exposed surface with scraping tools, cutting and scraping away loose flesh, fat, and membranous connective tissues. This for several hours. Then she flipped the skin over and re-staked it, stretching it further than it had been drawn out before. She again painstakingly scraped it, gradually, inch by inch, working all the hair off its exterior.

The next step involved submerging the denuded skin into one of the seal skin vats that she had pre-filled with a potion made from mixing the deer's brain matter in nearly equal parts with brackish water that had been taken from the river during the last incoming tide. The skin was left soaking in that solution for the next day, being intermittently removed, wrung out, twisted tightly into various contortions and creasings, and then re-submerged into the liquid for further soaking, at regular intervals.

After a full day and night of soaking, Ah'necca removed it, re-stretching it and draping it over a self-standing tripod made from sturdy cedar sapling poles. She began to re-work the hide over the next several days as it dried, flipping it periodically to change the side exposed to the sun. With each re-set that stretched it further she would rub down its exposed side with more of the tanning mixture that she had earlier made from the brains.

After several days of this, she built and reduced a campfire, setting greens on it to generate smoke. She moved the tripod with the staked hide over to a position straddling the smoldering remnants of the fire. This began the final process of essentially smoking one side of the hide at a time, flipping it periodically to alternate the side being smoked, and re-setting the fire to maintain consistent heat and smoke as needed.

By the end of the final day, the hide was tanned. She rolled it up and tied it into a bundle that would be stored in a corner of the hut for now. It was still stiff and unworkable, but the rest of its preparation for being made into a garment for her family could now await a winter day. A quiet moment off into the future, when the rains would make indoor duties more desirable than outdoor ones. Then, she would take this project back out, unroll it, and again begin to work it with her hands, rubbing a concoction made from animal fat and smelt oil into it to soften it and make it pliable and pleasant to have against one of their bodies as protection from the elements.

chapter eight

POSSUM

ONE OF THE EARLIEST SPECIES OF *fauna to have graced the continent, opossums are indigenous to North America. Remains have been found that are literally millions of years old.*

Yet although native thereto, they are the only marsupial in existence on the North American continent.

Females are equipped with pouches and give birth to a remarkable number of "joeys" each year, with sometimes as many as twenty babies in a single litter. The ones of the Pacific coastal area are slow but courageous creatures, about the size of a raccoon; mostly mottled whitish grey in color other than a small black area around the eyes and a pink nose.

They are rarely seen in daylight hours. They are tree climbers with dexterous fingers and toes clawed for gripping bark and have strong long rat-like tails by which they can hang from branches. They have rather large ferocious looking canine teeth that may be quickly flashed with flair when one of these little creatures is provoked by any interested predator or passer-by.

But they generally are more likely to be eaten by people than to cause a human any serious concern.

Possums subsist on a diet of rodents, birds, eggs, frogs, plants, fruit and insects.

Po'la laughed.

His sister Ee'na had awakened him. It was still dark out. She was a mischievous child and had, just a moment before stepped out of the hut by herself in the night to urinate. Apparently, she had encountered something out there of much interest to her.

But she had already misbehaved by not waking a parent before going outside, so it was Po'la's advice she now needed in the matter.

She had pushed him repeatedly on the chest until, coming to consciousness, he had realized it was just her. He raised his hand to stop her.

Putting a finger to her lips in a shushing gesture, she grabbed his raised hand, and as he sat forward, pulled him upright, out of the hut and into the night.

The stars above were bedazzling, but Ee'na had no time for them. Pulling her brother along to where their afternoon meal had been earlier consumed, out by the place where the now-doused cooking fire had earlier burned.

It was a possum. Its ambling movement as it was making its way to the edge of the village had brought on Po'la's reaction—a mirthful sense of relief, expressed merely as a chuckle.

His father had taught him about these strange creatures just months before during a night-training hunt.

This one was a mother, which they realized as they trotted up closer to it. Literally covered in babies that were clinging tightly with little tails and claws intertwined into the mother's fur.

Po'la knew that possum meat was edible, if not at the top of the list of the most desirable animal foods. But both children also already knew that one must never kill more than is necessary to cover the needs of the family and the tribe. Such was a serious offense to the spirits. And Po'la quickly realized that killing this mother would ultimately also, even if he and Ee'na spared them, eventually result in death for all the babies, and they were many.

But he did want his sister to see something that his father had shown him on the night they had encountered another possum, one with no babies. What a possum does when it feels threatened.

Unfortunately for it, the outcome for that other little animal, the one Po'la had met in his first encounter with the species, had come out differently than would be the case for its counterpart in this night's adventure.

Po'la gently grasped his sister's shoulders and moved her behind him, taking her hand and leading now, and then advanced to a position nearer the possum. It realized they were approaching, stopped waddling away, and pointed its beady-eyed little face directly at them.

Stopping Po'la and Ee'na in their tracks.

It had, just as he had expected, elected to stand its ground and fight. It sneered up at them, seemingly fearless. Its lips pulled back, exposing canine-like fangs. With saliva dripping from its mouth. Hissing and growling ominously.

The children jumped back a step. They stood there, watching it from what they felt was a safe distance. Her babies squirmed restlessly on the mother possum's back in an undulating pattern that made it look like the adult creature's skin was crawling.

The kids suddenly remembered they were out in the night without the knowledge and protection of adults. They left the brave mother possum to her brood, snuck back into the hut, and quietly climbed into their respective layers of bedding.

Her mission of feeding on remnant off-castings from the villagers' afternoon meal having been modestly successful, the mother possum and her babies retreated, deep within the woods.

There, they were hanging from a high branch of a big leaf maple tree well before the first tentative fingers of light from the great yellow orb had begun to splash pink against the smattering of clouds that decorated the morning horizon.

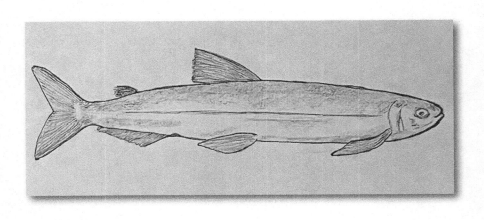

chapter nine

EULACHON

F OR THE LOWER RIVER PEOPLE, AND *many of the upriver tribes as well, the great fish runs of the Columbia River—varying species moving through it at different times of the year— were the primary food source year-round. These fish runs included five Pacific salmon species, as well as steelhead (sea run rainbow trout), sea run cutthroat trout, white and green sturgeon, smelt, and the lamprey eel.*

The smelt that pass annually up the Columbia River (eulachon), roughly six inches in length each, are adults headed to spawn in the lower reaches of several of the river's various tributaries. Like other anadromous species, they spend most of their lives in the ocean, make their remarkable passage back to their natal rivers after three or more years in the salt, and then die after spawning. Their diet in the ocean consists largely of plankton and krill, making them an oily fish that has been called the "candlefish" because, when dried, they can be lit by a flame or a hot coal from a fire, after which they will burn for a remarkable period, much as does a candle made of wax. Although they have been reduced to a threatened species status in our present-day world, historically the banks of the Columbia River would be littered with literally millions of dying and dead spawned-out smelt, just after the peak of an annual run which would typically occur in the heart of winter. They have long-been an important source of food for the indigenous people of the Pacific Northwest.

>—⋅>>

The rain had not let up for days. Po'la was stir crazy. It seemed he had spent most of the days this winter inside the hut, cooped up with his noisy little sister. She endlessly trying to annoy him into playing shell games or provoking him into another wrestling match. They were allowed to spend a few hours every third day in the large community hut, where along with other village children, they would be told stories by the elders about their grandfathers' and grandmothers' lives, the spirits whose ways and whims had always and would ever continue to influence their own past, present, and future, and given instruction in the law and traditions of the tribe.

It was expected that the children's parents would teach them the day-to-day basics of living life in the village. How best to drink, eat, bathe, sleep, forage, fish, hunt, trap, prepare and cook food, skin and butcher game, preserve fish and meats, tan hides, make garments, and fight to defend themselves.

It was a given that the warriors of the tribe would teach certain of the village children as they grew up how to use weapons and engage in battle at a more sophisticated level— the children that showed promise as combatants.

But all of that still left a gap in the overall development of tribal youth, which it remained for the elders of the tribe to fill. Essentially, it was the village elders that were expected to lend a historical, spiritual, tribal rules, and traditions bent to the education of the children of the village.

But, Po'la felt he had already heard enough of the elders' stories this winter. From his point of view, no more were necessary. And on this day, which was not one of the children's scheduled school days, he had been deprived of even that unspectacular diversion.

When Alouk returned from a morning's solo hunt empty-handed, dripping wet and shaking from cold exposure, Po'la quickly offered his father a hand in getting dried off and into warm buckskin garments. He then cautiously suggested that, when his father was warmed up and dried out, perhaps they should go out as a family and check to see if the eulachon were up in the river yet.

Alouk had at first just smiled at the boy. Going back outside did not sound appealing. But then, after a moment's further reflection, he had agreed. Ee'na squealed with delight when Alouk finally assented. Ah'necca laughed at the children's enthusiasm over something as simple as a family stroll along the river. The kids really needed to get outside!

Any further discussion at that point, however, was drowned out by the sound of rain, beating hard against the stretched leather of the hut's roof, above their heads.

Just before dark, as if the spirits had been listening earlier, there was a lull in the rain. It was still drizzling outside, but not heavily. The family stepped out of the hut and sauntered down to the river, the kids scampering about excitedly.

They walked its bank for quite a distance, as it turned out. All the way up to the mouth of the small tributary that entered just east of the village, which at this time of the rainy season didn't seem so small. Its drainage was coming into the great river hard, brown, and roily. Its raging waters were much deeper than was typical and brought to an end the little family's upstream progress.

Along the way they had all watched the riverbank closely for any evidence of the small silvery fish that at any time would suddenly inundate the river, swarming by, swimming upstream—shallow and accessible—in tremendous numbers. Ribbons of life making their way up the great river to spawn in backwaters and tributaries.

Po'la had found just two eulachon on a section of sandy beach. Ee'na only one, hers having been cast up on a cobbly stretch of gravel that they had passed just before arriving at the angry creek.

The parents had observed the kids dashing, competing to see who could first grab each tiny fish, with some degree of amusement.

But there was a more sobering thought that had struck both Alouk and Ah'necca, although they did not mention it. The presence of the three little fish signaled that within a day or so, soon anyway, the body of the eulachon run would begin to pass through. Which meant that the tribe's most important winter assignment would begin in earnest, and that they would find themselves working throughout the daylight hours, day after day until the run was past, no matter how bad the weather.

Brushing that thought aside, before they began to walk back to the hut, Alouk took the three little fish from the children and kneeled in the gravel along the shallows. He dipped his hand holding the smelt into the water, swirling it around several times, and then showed each child, in turn, how to slit the bellies and discard guts and reproductive organs. Handing back to each child their respective catch after he had cleaned and gutted the fish, he suggested to Po'la and Ee'na that such meager portions might be best used by just being cut up and added into the family's afternoon stew. Or, he told them, you can ask your mother to teach you how to make three candles out of them.

Ah'necca had watched Alouk with satisfaction as he illustrated the simple fish cleaning process and talked patiently with their children.

She prayed to the spirits that when the real numbers of eulachon arrived in a few days the tribe's harvest of the run would be good, as the children's real education on the benefits of this plain looking little fish, and what the gift of its arrival meant to their people, could begin in earnest.

chapter ten

HOSTILES

POTENTIAL ANIMAL PREDATORS OF A COASTAL *tribe's members during this epoch of history would have included the grizzly bear and grey wolves that were still widespread over the
Oregon coast and in the region's inland forests, in addition to
the black bear, coyote, and cougar that still thrive there today.
Of course, as has often been true throughout human history
and remains true today, the primary danger to any given tribe
of primitive indigenous people—aside from starvation, exposure to the elements, and sickness—was the existence of other
people nearby whose differing cultural upbringing engendered
clashing beliefs and values.*

II·>

History had proven the need for the tribe to be solicitous. Pre-
cautions were thus a part of daily life. Although individual
warriors might go out on hunts or to set up trade meetings
with friendly nearby villages, and any tribal member or family
could visit the river and the excrement grounds as needed to
fetch water, bathe, or defecate, generally, a system of communal protection was inherent in the law of the tribe, and was
strictly followed. Specifically, other than on the short trips
anyone might make to the nearby river, at least one or two of

the warrior class always accompanied tribal members who embarked on any other excursion. Foraging parties, for example, were planned, not spontaneous, and were required to include two or more warriors carrying weapons who kept their focus maintained solely on protecting the foragers. Likewise, two or more warriors were kept on sentinel duty at the village every minute of every day and night, and it was mandatory that at least six additional warriors be always kept at hand within the village, ready at call should a sentinel ever signal concern.

But they were not a large tribe. And all risk was not entirely preventable.

This was evident near the end of an otherwise rather pleasant day, early one year during the changeover from winter to spring. The weather had shifted from the unpleasant grind of the rainy season and the tribe was enjoying the emergence of a day of sunshine and warmth. But the whale meat was gone, and the collective tribal supply of dried fish was low.

Ty'ee called a meeting, decided to split the village warriors up, and sent Alouk out with six other warriors on a multi-day hunt. This left the village defended at only minimum strength, with just two sentinels, along with Ty'ee himself and six other "on-call" warriors remaining behind.

Of course, anyone and everyone in the village could use a weapon of some sort with at least some modest degree of efficacy, right down to the smallest child and the oldest of the elderly. The degree of experience and effectiveness of deployment was what separated the warriors from the others.

‖›

Ah'necca was not a warrior. She could wield a club and was capable with a knife, but her first baby had come along while she was still relatively young, and consequently she did not get much of an opportunity to train with spears or for warfare. Likewise, most of the other women of the tribe.

Elish'tie was another story altogether. As a child she had been kidnapped by hostiles and forced to work as a slave in an upriver camp of her captors. She had suffered much physical abuse and horrible indignities at their doing, but being resourceful she was always able to scavenge sufficient food and as each day of her captivity passed her limbs strengthened, hard work toning them.

Her body had at last caught up with her clever mind and indomitable spirit. Her captors sensed she was unlike the other captives they had taken and long held, who had become resigned to their fate as slaves. The insolent resignation Elish'tie always wore on her face as she worked with the others foreshadowed that she would break away if not kept under careful watch.

But doing so was a difficult task, and one day, when the eyes of her tormentors had briefly strayed elsewhere, she was able to smuggle a knife into her cloak. She hid it away.

She then waited. For the right one-on-one situation.

The opportunity soon came, as a male guard who had long been especially cruel to her awoke her from her sleeping place amongst the other slaves and pulled her into his empty hut, ignoring her angry pushback, overpowering her resistance.

Her smuggled knife came out, and her tormentor was soon silenced by it. She pulled back the fold of the hut, and the camp was now quiet. No one had heard their struggles, or if they had, apparently had misunderstood the reason for the grunting, thudding, and groaning.

Her guard's sacrifice gave her the head start she needed. Hiding by day and following the river downstream only during night hours, she had instinctively if not consciously retraced the way that her kidnappers had taken her when they tore her from her dying mother's grip, several years before, shattering her childhood and plunging her headlong into a world of abuse.

Her progress was slow in the dark. As the days added up, to dull her hunger she ate grubs and earwigs picked out from under rotting tree falls and sliced off a strip of her ragged buckskin garment and chewed on it. She drank from the river as needed to slake her thirst, and waited for the moonlight to reveal a landmark that would signal for her that she was back near her birthplace.

One morning, at first light, a village sentinel spotted and confronted her, and brought her in.

After her return, she did not confide in any of the tribe's people about the details of her terrible experiences that had occurred outside their realm. But all the village adults knew at least this much of her history—that she had showed up one day back in the village, several years after her abduction. No longer a child, but now a tall, sinewy young woman of striking appearance. With blood stains covering her tunic, and fire in her eyes.

Immediately upon her reappearance in the village, her parents having been slain when the hostiles attacked and took the girl, Tyée's woman had taken Elish'tie in to live with her and the chief. Their own efforts over the years before this to have children having met with death and sorrow, they were open hearts, ready to share their hut, their food, and their lives, with Elish'tie. They had embraced this hardened former captive of the hostiles, becoming her new family and providing her with a re-education in the ways of the tribe.

As the villagers came to know her again, they soon realized that this Elish'tie was quiet, actually, taciturn. She still recalled and was fluent in the spoken language of the village, but it seemed she would only use it when she had immediate need to accomplish something important by talking.

As she became an adult, another thing that Elish'tie received from Ty'ee (besides an adopted family and a home) was guidance in warrior training. No doubt, with having lived through being a slave over several of the formative years of her life, Elish'tie was hungry for whatever opportunity might be had now to strengthen herself and gain superiority in the ways of self-defense and battle. And Ty'ee, a mature warrior of great stature, was not just as good of a teacher as any, the truth was, he was at that time the best in the village.

And so Elish'tie became a designated warrior within the tribe.

Shortly thereafter with no other males in the tribe willing to even approach her despite her beauty, no doubt due to the reputation she had for being dour and physically intimidating, Elish'tie accepted Tilkeshi, also a warrior, as her mate.

‖·>

The nearby proximity of hostiles was first detected by Il'mec-ma, as he was returning from a day hunt. His hunt had been marginally successful. He had the carcass of a gray fox across his shoulders as he returned home.

But suddenly he realized that there was something not right. It hit him as he was passing through the next to last section of woods that led up to the village.

It was approaching evening, and typically in this moment of the day the crows that lived in that section of the woods would be inactive, settling into the roosts that they would keep over the course of the night. But some distance behind him, to his right and off in the trees, a crow was scolding something. To his left, again about the same distance back, several other of the birds were agitated. His own passage below the canopy should have been the only thing provoking their interest, but something else in the woods behind him, or several something or someone elses, was keeping the large black birds preoccupied, such that they were not paying Il'mecma any heed whatsoever.

Beyond that, however, Il'mecma could see nothing amiss, and he could not smell anything unusual. Still, the crows' behavior alone was compelling.

He hurried ahead and, catching the attention of and announcing himself by sign rather than call to one of its sentries, entered the village.

He dropped the dead fox at the door of his hut and hurried to alert Ty'ee to his concerns. Within minutes, word was spread throughout the warriors on call, weapons had been taken in hand or passed out, and the villagers were being pressed to gather at the center of the village, near to but outside of the large community hut. As the bunch there gathered, Ty'ee directed their positioning—elderly and children in the center, with other able-bodied adults in the secondary ring surrounding the most vulnerable, weapons bristling. Ty'ee and the on-call six warriors, including Elish'tie, Tilkeshi, and Il'mecma, soon to be joined by the two sentinels who had been summoned in from their posts, formed the exterior ring.

They did not have to wait long. Eight men brandishing spears and clubs, having realized their element of surprise had been taken from them, suddenly burst into sight at one end of the village. Screaming and howling, having worked themselves into a rage that could spell nothing but death for at least some.

Just moments later six more hostiles crashed out of the undergrowth at the other end of the village and began to rush in.

The first exchange, of spears as the ranks closed to a tight enough distance for them to be effective, felled Ty'ee, along with three of the hostiles. At that point, the fight immediately translated into a brutish scene of hand-to-hand combat. Spears now being used in-hand as lances, bludgeons falling, knives swinging and hacking. Men and women and children screaming in terror, rage, and pain.

Ty'ee down, three of the hostiles made it through the village's outer ring of warriors and began pulling at women and children to break them free of the village's defensive circle. Two grabbed Ah'necca as she was flailing at them with her club and knife, disarmed her, and started to drag her away. Her children saw this and it was too much. Both broke out of the protective enclave at the center of the bunch to go to their mother's aid. Another of the women in the second ring was able to grab and pull back Po'la, but little Ee'na took hold onto Ah'necca's leg and clutched it tightly, even as her mother was jerked away by the hostiles.

Elish'tie and Il'mecma and five of the village's other warriors stayed on their feet, their wounds not disabling, fighting like animals. They were barely managing to hold back the onslaught of hostiles at the front of the ring. They had caught peripheral glimpses of the back side of their defensive ring being ripped open and penetrated by the enemy. They saw and heard captives even as they were being taken, but as they were overwhelmed with trying to hold off the attack at the front, were powerless to do anything more than what they were doing.

Another of Elish'tie and Il'mecma's warrior brethren went down, badly hurt. Elish'tie felled the hostile that was towering over him, just as he was raising up to drive home a fatal blow. Delivering a single deadly blow with her club to the back of the hostile's head.

Then, even more suddenly than the enemy had appeared, its surviving combatants abandoned the fight and fled.

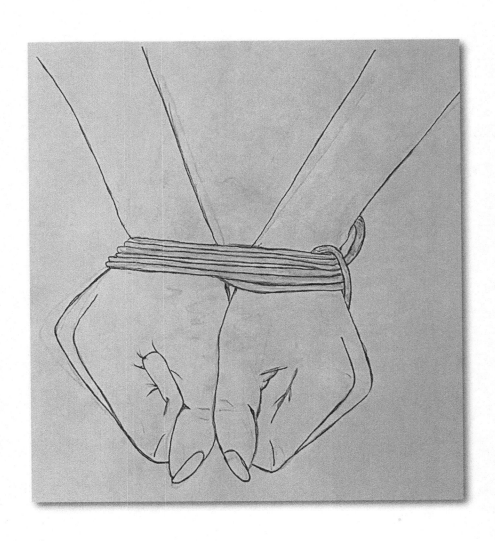

chapter eleven

RESCUE

In THIS EPOCH OF HUMAN EXISTENCE, *just as there always have been (and as remains true yet today), there were bands of people that were friendly to each other, and there were those that were bitter enemies of one another.*

Somewhere in the painful past of our tribe, long before Ty'ee became its chief, a large upriver band of nomadics—which Alouk and Ah'necca and their people knew only as the hostiles—began a pattern of systematic attacks on Ty'ee's and other coastal tribes. Randomly raiding the victim tribes' stores of food and other supplies when they might luck upon a poorly guarded village, and occasionally trying to overwhelm a defended village. The aspect of the raids which was most horrifying to the members of the peaceful coastal tribes was the hostiles' practice of stealing women and children, which they would subject to slavery, or kill if they became more trouble than they were worth to the hostiles.

)⋯≫

Ty'ee was dead, the spear that had taken him down having severed a major blood vessel in his upper thigh. Around him lay the bodies of three hostiles.

Tilkeshi and another of the village's downed warriors, Mane'ilhte, were alive but had suffered disabling wounds. They could be of little help, at least for the time being.

Il'mecma and the remaining standing warriors gave her their blessing, and Elish'tie assumed command. She would mourn Ty'ee later.

Two women and a child had been dragged away from their village. Ah'necca and Freya, and little Ee'na. The thought of what would happen to them did not sit well with Elish'tie. She knew all too well.

Il'mecma would stay behind and bury Ty'ee while the elders tended to the wounded. Hopefully Il'mecma's presence, with the support of the clubs and knives of the remaining mothers of the tribe, would be sufficient for the protection of those remaining within the village as it awaited the return of Alouk's hunting party, which was expected back at any time.

Elish'tie and the five other village warriors that were still able to travel and fight grabbed up several leather packs which they stuffed lightly with dried fish, took their weapons in hand, and launched in pursuit of the retreating band of hostiles and its three captives.

They were quick about it and struck out after less than an hour's delay. The trail was clear, one or more of the murderous bandits must have been bleeding profusely, and no doubt Ah'necca and the other kidnapped village mother were resisting and had to be dragged along or, like Ee'na, trussed and carried.

Fatigued from the strenuousness of the earlier battle, but not exhausted, Elish'tie and her men moved at a brisk jog.

Single file, she in the lead, running but in a reserved fashion, as silently as possible. Her ears attuned ahead. Her eyes riveted to the signs of disturbed brush and occasional blood splatters which kept her confident that their quarry was not far ahead.

They caught up with the group of hostiles as twilight began to steal light from the sky. She was grateful, as tracking in the dark would have been tedious and slowed her rescue party measurably, robbing it of its main advantage—speed.

It was the sound of the child's crying that she had first perceived, barely noticed over the sound of her own controlled breathing as they were jogging. She slowed and signaled a halt. They all paused, and while catching their breath, heard a slapping sound some distance ahead of them, several whimpering noises, and then quiet.

She did not let her group blunder up on the hostiles, not even attempting to get close enough for a visual. She did not want any of the three captives at risk of being sacrificed, or to create any situation where they could be used as shields or hostages for negotiation purposes.

They gathered, slowing their advance to a silent crawl, proceeding forward just enough to remain out of sight but within earshot of the occasional growling voices and softly thudding foot sounds emanating from the band ahead of them.

Complete darkness came on rapidly. It was a moonless night. Elish'tie did not know if the hostiles would encamp or keep moving, but she assumed the latter, and didn't wait to find out.

As a child, she and other women and children that had been captured by the men of these hostile tribes had compared their experiences. It had surprised Elish'tie to learn that retaliation by the raided villages was rare, and generally unsuccessful even when it did occur. She knew that her village, in response to the attack of this day, had already done more to protect its people than these brutes would have expected. She was confident that the men ahead of her were of a belief that they were not now being followed. That they had left her tribe in a such a state of shock, disarray, and mourning that pursuit would not even be considered. Or when it finally was, that it would be too late for its warriors to pick up their trail and seek the rescue of the captives they had taken.

She and her men were six strong, but with surprise on their side now. Against what she held in her head from the memory of the fourteen hostiles that had rushed in during the opening attack, less the three dead men they had left behind and whatever further degree of weakness might benefit the rescue effort due to one or more of the hostiles having suffered more severe wounds than had she and the village men now with her. She had seen, as the attackers had fled, at least two of them having to be held up, a man under each arm, helping them to scurry out of the village. So, by her calculations, the enemy's strength was essentially down to nine left that would have to be beaten or killed in the upcoming fight.

She split her men into two groups which separated and fanned out, pressing suddenly more abruptly ahead, but wide of the location through which they believed the enemy was continuing to move, intending to flank the hostiles. If in the darkness they were able to get close enough and discern who was where, to be certain enough that their targets were enemy and not the three they were there to recapture, then their spears would lead the attack. No word or signal would be spoken or given. Quite simply, when she was ready, El-ish'tie would just loose her spear. The thud of it landing into the body of one of the attackers would trigger five more such missiles raining down upon the hostiles, with the six rescuers leaping in immediately behind the spears.

She slipped ahead silently, two village warriors behind her. She could make out several of them now as they came through a clearing not far from her location. Several men unencumbered in the front, followed by a small group of people clumped together, seemingly holding onto each other, and a single person, alone, bringing up the rear.

At that moment, the enemy band with its captors paused. Elish'tie waited. She was easily within range, and had room enough around her such that, upon rising, she could accurately throw her spear, but she wanted to be sure that that the hostiles hadn't pushed one of the adult captives into the front or the back of their grouping. Then she heard the two female voices exchange whispers, and it was clear that they were there, with the child, in the center of the group. It was time. She rose, delivered her spear into the man standing alone closest to the captives, and as he screamed and clutched at his chest, Elish'tie leaped forward, scrambling over the brush that had covered her position, with her club in her hand.

Two other hostiles dropped with fatal spear wounds, other thrown lances from her men having had their desired effect, before Elish'tie was able to engage. She did not realize it at that moment, but the odds were suddenly even. Six able-bodied villagers versus six able-bodied hostiles.

Their hands and ankles bound tightly with leather straps, the captives could do nothing to help. At first, in the darkness and still reeling from the earlier violence and shock of their plight, Ah'necca could not grasp what was happening. Once she grasped that their kidnappers were under attack, she remained anxious and fearful until she realized that these spirits that had emerged from nowhere out of the darkness were her own people.

Elish'tie had gone in like a banshee, slamming her bludgeon into the shoulder of one hostile, crushing it and dispatching him with a follow up slash of her obsidian knife. Instantly leaping from there onto the back of another, raising her knife high as she positioned to drive it down and disable him. He instinctively dropped to his knees and fell backwards onto her, but it was too late. Before he could dislodge her from his back she had driven her blade deep into his neck.

She had disabled two of the six hostiles remaining within seconds. Her five warriors engaged with the other four hostiles, she rushed to the side of Ah'necca and cut the bonds that were restraining her limbs. Without having said a word, she did the same for Ee'na and Freya.

The skirmish was over almost before it had begun. Another of the hostiles had been killed when overpowered by two of Elish'tie's warriors, and three hostiles had realized the tide had turned on them and simply fled. Disappearing into the night screaming howls of rage.

Elish'tie surveyed the wounds on the two hostiles that had been disabled in the earlier battle, only one of which was conscious at all, and barely so at that, and determined that they would not be recovering soon, if ever. She did not recognize these two, and suspected they were of a different camp than the one in which she had been forced to live entrapped over the latter years of her childhood. Still, these were mortal enemies of her people, and they had just killed her adopted father—the chief of her people—and seriously wounded her mate, Tilkelshi and another warrior of her tribe. Tribal tradition dictated that she do it herself or have her men kill them, and she knew she had every reason on a personal level to act accordingly. But she did not do so. Their fate, she decided, would instead depend on the fortune of how their wounds impacted them and whether their own people elected to try to come back for them. She let them lie on the ground and turned her attention again to the captives, ready now to speak with them.

Ah'necca, Ee'na, and Freya had superficial cuts in places from where the leather cords had bound them and were starting to show bruising from having been repeatedly slapped. But they were alive. Elish'tie only told the mothers that none of their children had been hurt or killed during the attack of the hostiles. She left out the news of the death of Ty'ee and of the wounded status of her own Tilkeshi and Freya's man. The women were already shaken, and all would be known soon enough. Right now, she needed them as sane, function-al, and focused as possible.

She pressed the rescue party to return all the way back to the village that night. They were more than willing, all wanting, before the light of morning broke, as much distance between them and the hostiles as possible.

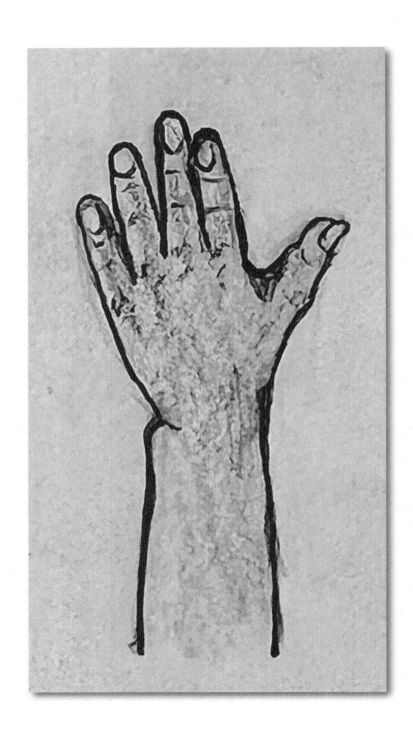

chapter twelve

ELECTION

THE SUDDEN AND UNEXPECTED LOSS OF *a tribe's chief could leave it dysfunctional and hence particularly vulnerable. Who might fill that void, and how they should be chosen, was the tribe's crisis of the moment.*

Despite the relative success of the tribe's defense strategy and rescue effort, the vicious battle with the hostiles had ended up being a costly one for the tribe. The non-fatal injuries to tribal warriors other than Tilkeshi and Mane'ilhte amounted to little more than superficial gashes and bruises, none of which appeared to be life-threatening. But Tilkeshi's injury was bad, and he was being cared for in the community hut by the most capable of the village healers, an elder by the name of Mikalia. After enduring the painful experience of her having, with Elish'tie's assistance, straightened a grotesquely broken leg and getting a jagged knife wound in his upper back cleaned and dressed, Tilkelshi had finally lapsed into a deep sleep. At that point, Mikalia had pushed Elish'tie away. "He must rest now", she said. "Go and tend to the business of the village. This is a difficult time for our people."

It was indeed. Ty'ee's body lay in repose in his hut, with Elish'tie's adopted mother at his side. Not just his woman and their daughter, but the entire tribe was mourning him.

In addition to the loss of its beloved chief, the tribe had sacrificed another brave warrior in defending itself. Freya's man, Mane'ilhte, who had been badly wounded as two hostiles had overwhelmed him as he tried to stop his mate, the mother of their three children, from being pulled away by the hostiles. He had then died in the night from his wounds.

Having returned to find him dead, Freya was now in complete and utter shock, alone in her hut with her children and their father's body.

Having been shooed from the side of her own man, Elish'tie went first to the hut of the dead warrior to see Freya and her children. She spoke softly with Freya whom, perhaps because of the trauma of the abduction and battering she herself had suffered, did not appear able to accept that Mane'ilhte's spirit had passed. Elish'tie gathered the three little children up and took them to a neighboring hut, receiving assurances that they would be looked after by the family there for the time being. She then visited her adopted mother at Ty'ee's side, her heart sad, but her mind active, attuned to the responsibilities she knew lay ahead, which her father was no longer there to be able to handle.

This was the state of his people, when Alouk and the hunting party returned. They were greeted by a somber village.

Learning what had happened and that Ah'necca and the children were in his family's hut, Alouk went directly in to see them. He did not emerge for quite some time.

It was Il'mecca that summonsed the warriors and put out word that the time for assembly had arrived.

Soon Elish'tie and Alouk and their warrior brethren, the elders, and adults of the village other than Tilkeshi, Freya and Ah'necca, had all come together in the place of assembly, ready to be addressed.

Once he believed all had been seated, Il'mecca stood and began speaking. Today, he said, we mourn the passing of the spirits of Ty'ee and Mane'ilhte. He extolled their accomplishments and lamented their loss. He noted the loved ones they had left behind, and spoke of his intent, as he expected of all in the tribe, to ensure that the beloved of Ty'ee and Mane'ilhte would never be alone or go hungry.

But he quickly pivoted to the question of leadership. He said the tribe had lost a great chief. The decision of who must permanently replace Ty'ee would have to be made. He paused for a moment, as if reflecting.

Then he continued, saying that there were in his mind but two people who should be considered—the tribe's two greatest living warriors. He nodded in the direction of Alouk and Elish'tie. As he pronounced their names, one after the other, the assembled villagers, without prompting, repeated each name in almost perfect unison.

Once the murmurs of the crowd faded out, Il'mecma called out abruptly, "Does anyone else lay claim?"

No one stepped forward. He scanned the assembled tribe carefully to make sure. No, the choice was to be just between the two.

Il'mecma went on. "The collective voice of the village", he said, "will decide."

He then continued, saying that Alouk had long been, at Ty'ee's designation, the top warrior in the village, and that his reputation for strength of mind, body, and spirit was legendary. Il'mecma suggested that Alouk would likely have been, were the old chief still alive to say so, Ty'ee's first choice as his successor.

But then Il'mecma shifted his gaze to the tall lean woman seated next to Alouk, whose face was a portrait of strength, confidence, courage, and wisdom, all at once. He paused his speech.

Elish'tie was watching Il'mecma, patiently, as if she knew—before he had even thought of it himself—what he was going to say. As if she was looking ahead at how the question of who should be the village chief would be answered, without having to wait for any of this to happen. As if she were already, in her mind, sorting out how the order of things would best be structured, assigned, and accomplished, from burying the dead, to healing Tilkeshi and the emotionally wounded captives, to preparing for the next food harvest, and on down the line.

Somehow, looking at Elish'ite comforted Il'mecma, as it did everyone whenever they were in her presence.

As if coming out of a momentary trance, Il'mecma turned his attention back to the people and resumed. "Now", he said, "Elish'tie, Ty'ee's adopted daughter, is likewise a warrior. And her reputation is nearly equal to that of Alouk."

He then proceeded to tell them that there were two additional things about Elish'tie that he felt deserved mention.

First, that the spirits had blessed her with the gift of "vision", as had been demonstrated repeatedly over the years. Tribal lore was replete with stories of her mysterious grasp of the metaphysical and wisdom far beyond her years. Her vision and advice had many times helped one villager or another in some not insubstantial manner.

Second, that the importance of her actions in defending the village during the attack by the hostiles could not be overstated. Her ferociousness and effectiveness in battle, and her courage in orchestrating and executing the rescue mission, had been exemplary.

Il'mecma waved out to the crowd. If anyone wants to add anything to what I have said before we settle upon a decision, I invite them to speak now.

No one offered. But then Alouk rose, prepared to speak. Il'mecma waved him forward and stepped aside.

Alouk began by addressing Il'mecma.

"I am honored at your words about me, my friend. Coming from a great warrior like you, they are especially gratifying."

He then nodded to the assembly and said, "I am grateful to all of you, also, for even considering me today as this question of who will be chief so suddenly, and tragically, confronts us.

"But there is no choice to be made here, as I am not seeking to be your leader. The simple truth is that there is another more capable member of this tribe ready and willing.

Elish'tie is the one and only warrior who can and will best serve this village as its chief, for as long as she may live. Even before today I knew that.

"But after learning what my beloved Ah'necca told me just before I walked from our hut to here, about the rescue that Elish'tie commandeered, I know in my heart, with unshakable certainty that it is Elish'tie, and not I, who must be our chief."

Alouk then spoke directly to Elish'tie. "The debt that Ah'necca and I owe you, Elish'tie, is so great that it could never be repaid. But I commit to serving you to the best of my abilities, however you may direct me to do so for the good of our village, for as long as I am alive and able."

He was done speaking.

Elish'tie stood and approached Alouk, took his hand, gripped it for a moment, and then released it. A good man, a great warrior, had given her his thanks, and his blessing. She was ready.

She faced the assembly.

"I would be honored to be your chief, if it is what the majority wishes. I will let you, the people, decide that. Il'mecma's words have moved me. Alouk's words have touched me deeply. They are both magnificent warriors. Capable and decent men. I think it is well known that I have a tremendous love for this village and all its people. I watch you raise your children to be kind but also strong and self-sufficient. I was, against my will, forced to live elsewhere once, amongst people who raised their young to hate and to prey upon others. I believe the spirits are and will always be with us. With this tribe, because we do not pillage others, and we kill only what we must to eat and feed our people. I want you all to know that I feel ready to lead, if asked. To lead the kind of people that you are. To be a part of helping this village survive and prosper. To protect it. To make sure that those who hate and would prey upon this village continue to be repelled and defeated at every turn.

"I have said enough. I will leave it to Il'mecma to discern if more discussion should be had and to put the final question to you as to who will be chief. I go now to join my adopted mother in bidding farewell to the spirit of our beloved Ty'ee."

As she walked to her mother and father's hut, she heard behind her the sound of her name being chanted by every voice that could speak in the village.

So it was that at the time of Ty'ee's death, Elish'tie became chief of the village.

chapter thirteen

ᚦREAM

FOR THE TRIBE, THE SHAKING OF *the mountains, followed by the arrival of great waves that overran beaches, filled rivers and valleys with salt water, and wiped out virtually every settlement situated in any low-lying coastal regions, was a thing of legend only. But this was only because it had been several hundred years since such an event had occurred as of the time that Alouk and Ah'necca lived along the Pacific Coast. The memories of those few who had survived the last great quake had been passed down as stories from generation to generation, but after those then-living had all died off, with each retelling of the tale the stories had become less vivid in description, and hence less easily perceived by the new listeners as anything that might ever haunt the tribe or its children over the course of their lifetimes.*

Believed by all in the village to be connected to the spirits, Elish'tie was also known to be subject to premonitions, and for her premonitions to end up being a part of the tribe's reality. On one occasion, she had told a young couple that she had been watchful of their labors over the summer, and that although she was not dissatisfied with their efforts, she nevertheless felt that they should lay away more food than they had already collected. After they had listened, respecting her input, recruited assistance, and followed her wise counsel—working extra hard during the fish harvest in the fall—they were grateful that they had. A new child entered their hut the very next winter that had not been expected. And the extra food that Elish'tie had encouraged them to have on hand was more than put to good use. This, Elish'tie's sort of mystical sense of what was coming, had been illustrated again and again as events played out in the village.

Now, three springtime's had come and gone with Elish'tie as the chief of Alouk and Ah'necca's tribe.

One day she told the villagers of a dream that had awakened her in a sweat the previous night, filled with fear and great sadness. In her dream, she and all the village had perished, inundated under a land bound mass of ocean water that had drowned everyone. All the following day she wept for the village, until she had no tears left.

And then she decided to do something about it.

Had it been any other of the tribe's members, even any one of the more influential ones, it surely would not have been enough to trigger the actions and extraordinary labors that next occurred. But Elish'tie's reputation for wisdom, and her people's belief that the spirits spoke with and through her, made a difference.

At her insistence, the healed Tilkeshi, who could walk but not run or hunt any longer, went out over the next several days, assisted by two younger warriors, exploring higher elevation possible village sites. Potentially suitable locations were marked, and then visited by Elish'tie one by one, until she was satisfied. The right place had finally been found. It was less than a half day's walk from their existing village. There was an ample clearing for the relocation of the community and its various individual huts. Access to the river was not a problem. But much had to be done to create temporary dwellings at the new site that the tribe's people could stay in as their old village was broken down and rebuilt at its new location on higher ground.

The work was hard. There was much grumbling but no serious dissension. Unfortunately, as it turned out, there was more than the usual amount of hunger experienced by tribal families the ensuing winter, because over the spring, summer, and fall preceding it so many in the tribe had focused their labors on the relocation project instead of provisioning for the winter ahead.

But sharing was a part of the village culture, no one reached the point of starvation, and eventually, before the new buds of springtime were blossoming, all was done. Every man, woman and child, young and old, whether they be warrior or lesser tribal member, had access to a safe structure, temporary at least, in which to pass the upcoming winter.

And just like that, the tribe had moved, reestablishing itself in its new home on the side of a mountain that was still close to the river, but at a substantially raised elevation from sea level.

And finally Elish'tie slept, now in her old bedding at the new village site, the deep sleep of a leader content in the knowledge that the spirits were pleased with her people.

chapter fourteen

GRIZZLY

T HIS WAS A TRIBE THAT WAS *proud. Self-sufficient—its people always had ample water, and typically were well fed and
healthy. The children and the elders were always kept under
the protection of strong and able warriors. They were settled in
a strategic, permanent location and had constructed shelters
sufficient to protect all members from the elements. The ways,
traditions, and rules of the tribe were valued, respected, and
passed down from generation to generation.*

*There were some goods, however, that were not available or
at least were less plentiful on the coast, that were occasionally obtained by trading with certain inland tribes of a friendly
inclination. Surplus dried or smoked fish (usually salmon and
smelt) and various cockle clam and other seashells could be
useful as barter to exchange for goods from non-coastal tribes.
In return, wild leeks and onions (which grew more plentifully
in interior regions), acorns, Pacific crabapple fruit and bark
(used for medicinal purposes), dried huckleberries, smoked
fish (other than salmon and smelt, such as lamprey eel or sturgeon), jerked red meats (bighorn sheep, buffalo, antelope, or
bear), and chunks of obsidian rock (for making knives and
spear heads) might be taken back by the tribe. Other items that
might be offered by either party to a transaction might include
simple baskets woven from pine needles or plant fibers; clay*

pots of differing sizes and shapes; leather goods including slings and pouches, packs, water vessels, moccasins or garments; pre-made clubs, spears, knives, adzes, or hatchets; or ornamental wear (necklaces, bracelets, or hair pieces of various sizes and styles made from agates, seashells, fine bones, bird feathers, or a combination of the above).

The trading involved simple barter. A tribe wanting or needing something specific would initiate the idea for a transaction by sending a messenger to a tribe who in the past had been a reliable trade partner and a known supplier of the desired goods. The messenger would visit the other tribe and, if it were confirmed that both sides had surplus goods and mutual interest in an exchange, arrange a time and place for a meeting.

Elish'tie and Alouk were out fishing with two other hunters in the dugouts. It was late in the fall, after much of the work from the great annual salmon harvest had concluded. While the tribe's catch from the fall chinook and coho run already had been substantial, the chief hoped to bring in and smoke at least another small catch of coho to have on hand for trade purposes.

Il'mecma, who had been on sentinel duty just outside the west end of the village, intercepted and then brought two emissaries from a friendly central valley tribe into Elish'tie's hut to meet with Tilkeshi.

They wanted fish and offered to barter various items in trade. Tilkeshi invited them to stay the night in the village. If

Elish'tie's hunting party were to return with a sufficient catch, he explained, then arrangements could be made for a meeting and exchange. If not, then he would defer to Elish'tie as to whether the tribe would be willing to part with any of their existing stores of preserved fish.

Elish'tie and her hunting party arrived back in the village after dark, as it turned out, with a decent day's catch. Three large chinook salmon and seven mature coho, gutted and ready to be butchered and smoked. A work party was organized that would build and light smoking fires, begin cutting up the fish, and continue processing the catch throughout the night and into the next day, until the meat was all preserved.

The visiting emissaries joined Elish'tie and her warriors in a celebration held to thank the spirits for the catch. The visitors bid farewell the following morning as they left to return inland to their homes.

Arrangements had been agreed upon. The meeting would occur at a midpoint rendezvous site roughly equal distance between the two villages. The type and quantity of foods and other items to be exchanged were all pre-negotiated.

The day before the anointed meeting date, Il'mecma, Alouk, and three additional warriors embarked on the trade mission. Four of them carrying packs on their backs loaded with the items to be traded, but one of them always remaining unencumbered and with weapons at the ready, as a guard for the group. At rest halts, the packs were switched, rotating from man to man, with the responsibility for guarding the mission likewise transferred. It ended up being slightly more than a day's walk, slowed as they were by having to haul the loaded packs. But they arrived at the designated site just after dark on the day before that which was set for the meeting.

Early the next morning, six men carrying their tribe's goods that were to be exchanged arrived. Salutations were exchanged. Mutual inspections of the respective goods occurred, the eleven men shared food and water together, and then Alouk and his companions loaded up their new bundles and began the journey back to their village.

They were about halfway back to the village. Il'mecma was in front on security detail as they progressed down a narrow deer trail. Behind him single file walked three other village warriors carrying bulging packs, Alouk bringing up the rear also heavily laden with goods.

Alouk heard the grizzly before he saw it. The grunt of a large animal moving rapidly at him, with the sound of air and slobber blowing from the bellows of its lungs. It was a gigantic male bear that had picked up their scent trail and followed it at a trot, until suddenly it had caught up, and came up behind them. By then, it was in full charge mode.

Alouk yelled. "Siam!" He had a spear and club in hand but could do little with either, as his arms were impeded by the straps holding the large bulky pack on his back. Nor could he run, duck, or jump with any degree of quickness or speed. But he knew his yell would bring four warriors back with weapons, so he did the only thing that seemed to make any sense. He turned to fight while writhing his shoulders up and down to try to shed the pack without losing hold of either the spear or the club. But the bear was on him before the pack shook down and he could get his spear raised.

Alouk twisted his torso at the last second as one of the grizzly's massive paws connected. The claws tore into the loaded pack, tearing it free of Alouk, and the force of the blow knocked him onto his back, down in the trail. The bear snarled and was straddling over him when suddenly it reared up, its attention focused on something new, some new concern in the trail just past Alouk. Il'mecma was there brandishing his spear at the bear, with the three other warriors doing the same, screaming at the bear, waving their weapons, in turn leaping toward the monster, then fading back, over and over.

The grizzly snapped and swung at the spears, as they came lunging toward it, one after another, and then were pulled back.

For a moment, Alouk's life hung in the balance. This great creature could have killed all of them before it ever succumbed to whatever inconsequential wounds the warriors' lances and clubs might be able to inflict upon it.

But the bear was not stupid. It realized now it would be a fight, and one that these men seemed to be more than willing to wage. To the death if need be.

The grizzly dropped down from its raised stance, whirled, and loped off, back in the direction it had come.

Alouk stood up, entirely unscathed. Without a word, he repaired as best he could the slashed but still functional pack, lifted it, rotated it over onto his back, and nodded to his warrior brethren.

They had to hasten along if they wanted to be within the relative safety of the village before nightfall.

chapter fifteen

RABBIT

IN PRIMITIVE TIMES, THERE WERE TWO *basic methods of snaring small game. The first and simplest, if it worked, caught the head or limb of an animal in a slip-cord which, anchored to a tree, rock, or a peg pinned to the ground, restrained the prey. A disadvantage to this method was that the small animal so entrapped would stay alive, struggling, until the snare was tended, and thus might have the opportunity to escape by biting through or breaking the restraining cord before the snare was checked.*

That method, as did the second approach, the spring snare, utilized a "noose" consisting of a cord that could be made from a three or four foot length of dried intestines or a thin strip of leather (oiled with smelt or animal grease to make it pliable), fashioned with a small slip-loop at one end. The small loop was tied with a circumference about the size of a modern-day nickel. The other end of the noose cord was tied off either to a tree or to a peg stuck in the ground when just the simpler snare system was being set. The noose end of the cord would then be opened into a circle (about the size of an adult's hand with all fingers spread out) and draped across twigs from low-laying branches along the trail at a location frequented by small game, perhaps to enter or exit their den or to seek food or water. When an animal passed partly into or through the open noose, as its body brushed the cord the noose would fall off the twigs and the loop would slip down, tightening the noose and restraining the prey from getting away.

The second method utilized essentially the same snaring cord apparatus but added a "spring" of sorts into the overall design—fashioned from a light branch like a willow sapling, placed under tension when the snare was set by being bent over to a significant degree. The hope being that the target would be jerked up into the air by the spring when the snare was triggered. Ideally, the animal would be killed instantly, with its neck snapped and its body kept well above the ground, thereby making it less susceptible to being pulled down and carried off by a coyote or other predator trying to get a free meal.

With the spring snare, the end of the cord opposite the noose was tied firmly to a short chunk of wood with a notch carved into it (or a forked willow branch) that served as the top half of a "trigger". A matching bottom piece of trigger, referred to as the "base" of the snare, was made from a slightly longer chunk of wood or forked willow branch, with its lower end whittled to a sharp point so that it could be sunk into the ground and its upper end carved into an opposing notch to be fit against the top half of the trigger. With the two halves of the trigger offset against each other at their respective notches, resistance could be maintained to keep the bent branch in place under tension until the snare was triggered. A leader line ran from the top part of the trigger up to the tip of the bent over sapling. The noose was then, again, set up by being draped in a fashion that would allow it to be easily pulled free from its set position by any animal passing partway into or through it. As the noose *tightened the top half of the trigger would be dislodged, the sapling would snap upright as the two halves of the trigger separated, and the spring trap was sprung.*

Occasionally, some of the snares were baited. What bait might be used depended on the game being targeted, for example, acorns might be put out if the target were grey squirrels, whereas dandelion greens or roots could be strategically placed if the plan was to snare rabbits. A small chunk of fish roe or entrails if the target were martin, ermine, otter, fox, raccoon, badger, possum or raptor.

What the target game might be depended on the particular area being set with snares—some types of small game being more concentrated at locations nearer a river bank, some types more common in meadows and at the edges of forests, and others, such as squirrels, more likely to be found deep within forested regions.

When supplemental meat was needed, or simply a change in taste from the drudgery of the tribe's usual diet, snares could be set and checked periodically during, and before returning from, foraging trips. Occasionally mothers and children might also, when other work was done, set and tend snares nearer the village, but because the rabbits and other small game along the river bank and living close to the tribe tended to get trapped out, those snares were rarely as productive as sets placed in and along the edges of the meadows and forests that were located more distant from home.

Ah'necca and Alouk had taught their children, as soon as they could walk and talk, how to set up and arm the snares that the tribe used for small game. Tending the snares, making the kill, and skinning and preparing small game had all been a part of the children's early education. Both Po'la and Ee'na were well-versed in all aspects of the process.

After her and her mother's abduction by the hostiles and the rescue, little Ee'na seemed to have irreparably lost her playful, childish personality. Ee'na insisted that her mother lie down with her each night at bedtime and hold her tightly. She would often scream in her sleep, or wake up in the night crying. In the daytime she was often sullen with her parents, and would lash out with fists in anger if her brother did not maintain a safe distance from her.

Her parents knew that Ee'na's having been in the midst of the violence of the battle during the hostiles' attack on the village, having been bound up and carried off by them, and then having to be a witness to the brutal beating of her mother as they were dragged away from the village during the hostiles' retreat, had all frightened their daughter horribly. Ah'necca herself was struggling with the emotional repercussions of all that had been inflicted on her daughter, herself, and her friend Freya, and couldn't shake the fearful thought of what would have happened if Elish'tie and the rescue party had not taken up such an immediate and courageous pursuit of the kidnappers.

Ah'necca felt she, being an adult, could deal with it. She and Alouk, however, were at wit's end as to what they might be able to do to help their daughter heal from the painful memories that were continuing to plague her. They had tried consulting with the elders regarding their daughter's aloofness, anger, and bad dreams. The wise ones' only advice had been that, with time, Ee'na's fears would recede. That in due course her parents could expect her to start to behave more like the child had been before the attack on the village had occurred. Much time seemed to have already passed, though. The parents were concerned that the expected spontaneous healing did not seem to be happening.

One day as spring rolled over into the early days of summer, warm but not yet hot out, the weather was particularly beautiful. The sun was shining. Grass shoots were emerging from the soil, dandelion flowers were beginning to open, and dragon flies were hanging suspended in the fresh air around the village as they searched for a mate. Alouk and Po'la were off on a training hunt. Ah'necca had Ee'na by the hand and they were out on a walkabout, checking four local snares that they had set earlier that morning before the family had eaten its first meal and split up to go separate ways.

There had been nothing in any of the first three snares that had been set earlier. As they had come upon and found each empty, Ah'necca had picked the snares up to take home with them after they had concluded making the rounds.

But as they approached the fourth and last, Ah'necca heard the rustle of leaves indicative of an animal in distress. They got closer and soon saw that it was a rabbit in the last snare.

It froze when it realized they were there, crouched, watching them.

Its body coloration was brown, with black and grey hairs interspersed throughout its pelt. Its ears, cocked back inquisitively, were long, the lighter brown around the edges of them fading into pink as the hair yielded to just skin at the center of each. Its eyes, mesmerizing, even from a distance—the irises a deep, beautiful brown, merging into black pupils at the center—stared imploringly up at Ah'necca and Ee'na. Just a tuft of its white tail was visible below its powerful back legs, bunched in readiness.

The cord of the snare was barely visible, but appeared to be wrapped around the rabbit's head and a front leg.

Ah'necca let go of her daughter's hand and took a quick step toward the rabbit, which instantly tried to bolt, but was slammed to a halt abruptly as it hit the end of the length of the snare cord that was restraining it. Ah'necca stopped, taking a step back to look around for a stick that could be used as a club. She had her knife on her but had forgotten to bring her bludgeon.

At that point, Ee'na stepped in front of her mother and held a hand up to stop her.

Ah'necca obliged, halting, suddenly curious of her daughter's intentions. It was not unusual for either of her children to take the lead and make the kill. That was what they had been encouraged by both of their parents to do in the past throughout the process of receiving their life-skills training.

But such wasn't going to be the case on this day.

The rabbit was again crouching, watching them, trembling, preparing to try to make another leap to safety.

Ee'na turned to face it. She put forward both of her little hands, as if displaying to the rabbit that she was not armed. She began to whisper quiet, soothing words. After several moments had passed, she stepped up, very slowly, to within reach of the rabbit. It raised its head up slightly and sniffed at the tips of the fingers on each of Ee'na's hands, one after the other; black whiskers on its cheeks twitching as if it were considering whether this unusual predator was about to end its life.

It must have decided not.

Ee'na bent slowly down, reached around it, and lifted it from the ground and into her arms. As she straightened up, she slipped the snare noose off its neck and leg and let the cord fall to the ground. She leaned her head over and gently kissed the rabbit on the tip of its ears, and then bent her knees and set the hare back down on the ground. Feeling the dirt below its sturdy back legs, it sprung away without a sound.

Ah'necca was surprised, but thought maybe she understood. They weren't starving and had plenty of smoked salmon left for the afternoon meal. She had herself, earlier, for just the flash of an instant, felt a strange impulse to let the rabbit go. There was something about it, something about the situation, that had upended her instincts and training, as she had first taken sight of it.

She looked at her daughter with wide eyes and felt an overwhelming sense of love and comfort. Ee'na had tears in her own eyes, but for the first time in ever so long, was smiling. Her mother took the child into her arms, and the two held each other for several minutes, without speaking.

Then Ah'necca gathered up the snare lying on the ground below them, and the two of them walked home.

That night, in the hut, Ee'na mischievously flicked her brother's ear, laughed, and was trying to scamper away from him when he grabbed her and wrestled her to the ground.

Seeing this, Alouk's eyebrow cocked up and he glanced at Ah'necca with a look of curiosity on his face. Ah'necca, however, was intent, just watching the children. Two kids, scrambling around on the dirt floor of the hut grappling for position, competing like bear cubs at play, as if nothing was unusual.

Perhaps the elders were right, Alouk thought to himself. All that it had taken for Ee'na to heal was time.

chapter sixteen

CONDOR

SOME FORTY THOUSAND YEARS AGO, LATE *in the Pleistocene epoch, the entire North American continent was a pleasant and fertile home for the second largest of our remaining flighted birds, the condor. It roamed the continent north to south and east to west during that era while America's great megafauna still stalked the landscape—mammoth, mastodon, camel, and giant sloth carcasses, among others—offering a plentiful supply of food for the winged scavengers.*

About 10,000 years ago, though, as North America's megafauna died off, the range of the condor correspondingly diminished. The loss of carrion from the greater beasts having reduced the condor's scavenging supply in the northern, midwestern and eastern regions of the continent. A robust population still flourished along the Pacific coast, however, from British Columbia down to Baja California, where its food supply of carrion from lesser beasts like dead deer, elk, and bear was supplemented by washed up carcasses of the larger marine species.

They are a magnificent flying machine. The wingspan of an adult condor may exceed 9 feet, and they can weigh more than 20 pounds. (Among the still-living bird species, the condor is second only to the albatross, the wayfaring ocean bird commanding the field with an 11-foot wingspan.)

Wild condors historically nested in rooks and caves on cliffs in the mountains, or occasionally in the trunks of giant sequoia trees. Their reproductive cycle is a delicate one, the female typically laying but one egg per season.

Unfortunately, now the breed is on the edge of the knife, so to speak, having nearly been wiped out by humans in the 19th and 20th Centuries. As the American frontier was settled, the condor was shot, poisoned, captured, and disturbed in its nesting grounds. Lead shot and other pollutant accumulations in the waterfowl carcasses it consumed contributed to killing it off, and its food supply of antelope, elk and other large wild animals was continually reduced by the encroachment of a modern destructive humanity into its previously wild habitat.

Just before the North American condor became completely extinct, a few dozen were taken into captivity, protected, and a breeding program was instituted. The entire world population had been reduced to just 27 birds.

The captive breeding program, a Southern California project, has been somewhat successful. By 2016, the population had grown to 446 birds. Release efforts, returning captive bred birds into the wild to try to repopulate the species into its previous range, were initiated in 1993. These releases have continued, reintroducing the birds into the wild in California, Arizona, Utah, and Baja California, in the years since.

As of mid-2024, there were reportedly 344 North American condors living in the wild, with another 217 in captivity.

〰

0600 hours
June 11
5,156 BC

The great bird sailed several thousand feet above the mouth of the river. Its bald head covered by an orangish-pink colored skin. A thin dull black color bar connected its beady black eyes, and a grey tip accented its sharp scimitar-shaped raptor beak. Its body and wing feather coloration was dusty black, while a large white triangle emblazoned across its chest extended out into the broadest section of each of its wings. In flight, as it was at this moment, it had the look of a black angel with a ribbed cape draped over outstretched arms, peering down from heaven upon an array of hapless earthbound creatures strewn out below it.

It was a clear cloudless morning. But surprisingly, at such an early hour of the day, with good winds. Sailing the skies in such conditions was nearly effortless for the condor. Soaring, riding the thermal updrafts, it could easily maintain altitude without needing to flap its wings.

The bird did not feel the shaking of the earth; it did not smell anything in the upper atmospheric air; it did not hear opposing Cascadia Zone tectonic plates grinding and forcing against each other far out at sea. It would have had no idea that the earth was being rendered and reshaped by an earthquake below the ocean's surface (one that would have measured at over 9.2 on the Richter Scale had modern science been around in such primitive times to measure it), had the bird's keen eyesight and incredible vantage point not caused it to pick up on the origination of the wave.

When its searching eyes first saw the wave form out in the Pacific Ocean, it was nothing more than a thin crease on the face of the half-blue planet below. Stretching north and south as far as the bird could see, that previously inconsequential crease soon rose high and formidable, and began to roll shoreward. The bird merely saw that the wave was moving rapidly; it could not appreciate that the huge column of water was advancing toward the beach at a speed of literally hundreds of miles per hour.

The condor was curious. It tilted the angle of its wing tips, gracefully dropping hundreds of feet in altitude in a matter of mere seconds, instinctively jockeying downward for a closer look. It had not seen anything like this happen before in its lifetime.

It stabilized there, at an altitude of some 500 feet above sea level. There it rode the wind currents safely as the great wave crashed below, rolling and breaking against the land.

The beach disappeared. The wall of water plunged inland, flattening even the most immense trees and immersing everything below its great wet mass.

The river mouth and the land surrounding it became an extension of the ocean itself. The condor's scavenging ground was gone, at least for the moment.

Inland a mile or two several mountain peaks remained in view, including the craggy cliff where the great bird's nest lay. Everything else below, however, was now just water.

The condor had become disoriented after the coastline disappeared. As it was endeavoring to drift in the sky inland toward its nesting area, nothing seemed right. The bird became anxious, as broken trees and debris tumbled and roiled about in the turbulent mess of sea water below it.

With a subtle change to the angle of its wings generating lift, it reascended to a higher viewpoint. For now, there seemed to be no option other than to just ride the winds of the upper atmosphere and continue to watch the unnatural events play out below.

Hours later, the sun now below the horizon and twilight softening the sky around the bird as it hung high up in the air, the condor apprehended that the sea water below had finally receded. A portion of the old coastline had again become visible. Littered along the cluttered remnants of beach, and even as far inland as the base of the mountain range, uprooted trees, tangled brush and other detritus was clumped about in piles everywhere. A plethora of dead animals, fish, and marine mammals lay haphazardly, motionless, across the lowlands.

All that was left of what had previously been the established villages of several lowland coastal tribes of people was a random collection of human corpses, lying prostrate along the river's edge; with several others grotesquely caught up in various root balls and on rocky structures stretched between the coast and the base of the interior mountain range.

With the old coastline visible and the river running again within its traditional bed, the great bird was finally able to reorient itself. Its wings aching with fatigue from having stayed aloft well beyond the duration of most of its normal hunting excursions, it flew toward its nest.

Near the base of the mountain, it observed various elk, deer, bear and other animals, these ones alive. Picking their way down the slope, descending, making their way back toward the desolate lowlands from which they had fled during the earlier shaking of the earth.

As it approached its nest, the giant bird's shadow passed momentarily over a small village of living humans; its residents moving excitedly about below. (These strange creatures had long been among the bird's neighbors, residing just below its nest on the side of the mountain.)

To the condor, the surviving villagers seemed unduly noisy, like a disturbed swarm of wasps or a scolding blue jay with an intruder about. The source of the humans' agitation could hardly have been appreciated by the brain of a bird, which had already forgotten the wave. Although the tribe's living structures that had been built halfway up on the side of the mountain were intact and their preserved food stores had remained undisturbed by the earlier encroachment of the ocean's waters across the lowlands, the people of this mountain village had seen what had just happened to the land below and were still anxiously absorbing what they had witnessed. They were terrified that the spirits might again unleash the anger of the ocean, which had just retreated literally from their doorstep, into their very midst. (It would, in fact, be several days before they could bring themselves to venture down the mountain to their beloved river to replenish their drinking water supply, bathe, and resume their daily rituals.)

Still, the great bird knew at least this much, that in the morning there would be plenty of food for it. There would be little if any competition when it alighted on its pick of the many carcasses gruesomely decorating the landscape below. The light of the next morning would bring for the condor an opportunity to feast unlike any it had ever known.

Content, it welcomed the darkness, and slept.

EPILOGUE

ODERN THINKING AS TO THE PATTERN *and trend of the shifting of the earth's tectonic plates, focusing here on the Pacific Coast of the North American continent which is the region known as the Cascadia Subduction Zone, has settled on a belief that great earthquakes, that is, of a magnitude of eight or higher on the Richter scale, are likely to continue to occur as they have historically occurred over the eons of time, on an average of about 570 to 590 years apart. The 9.2 Richter scale quake described heretofore in this story has been attributed by this author to a fictional date of June 11, 5,156 B.C., a date which falls within the known historical pattern of these multi-generationally spaced occurrences.*

Skipping ahead from the several centuries that followed immediately on the heels of the 8,000-years-ago-era in which this novel is set ultimately delivers us up to the doorstep of the most recent Cascadia Subduction Zone great quake occurrence, known as the "Cascadia Earthquake". It caused a massive tidal wave along the Pacific coastline of North America that wiped out many Native American settlements along with everything else in its path. It definitely was not a fictional event, having been historically documented to have specifically occurred on January 26 in the year 1700 A.D.

The scientifically documented earthquake and tsunami history commented on above suggests that if the statistical evidence simply based on averages bears out, the Pacific coastline will stay largely as it is, and not get wiped out by the next tsunami, until the year 2,280 or thereabouts—several generations removed from those alive in this 21ˢᵗ Century today, their children, and their grandchildren.

But the above numbers are merely based on averages. And the actual occurrence of a future seismic event is not necessarily accurately predicted just by looking back at historical averages. Indeed, sometimes the past large quakes of the Cascadia Subduction Zone occurred within only 300 years of each other. Other times, they happened as many as 900 years apart.

This is why some of the more progressive Oregon coastal communities of the 21st Century are already on an alert status. They have listened to "the wiser amongst us" of our time. Because if the next large quake occurs on the short side of being within the reoccurrence pattern, then a catastrophic event that will destroy communities and take countless lives could happen on the Pacific coast literally any time now.

The fact is, the tsunami threat has always been, from long before they lived and from Alouk and Ah'necca's tribe's time up to and including to today, all too real. With when it may happen next being ever the question, and the answer to that question being all too unpredictable.

The winter following the deaths of Ty'ee and the warrior Mane'ilhte, Il'mecma took the delicate Freya, who was by then struggling with the difficulties of unassisted mother-hood, on as his mate. Il'mecma made a good father and enjoyed being a part of raising Freya and Mane'ilhte's children.

Tilkeshi, although he survived his wounds from the hostiles' attack, unfortunately healed with a damaging loss of lower limb function. He was unable to ever again hunt or serve as a warrior. Though their bond always remained strong, the union of Tilkeshi and Elish'tie failed to produce any children. Tilkelshi's advice, however, was always sought and considered by Elish'tie as she continued to faithfully serve as leader of the tribe.

Alouk lived until after Po'la and Ee'na were grown, each had respectively found mates, and were raising families of their own. Alouk's reputation within the tribe as a hunter and warrior remained nearly unmatched until his death, which came suddenly and unexpectedly.

A hunting companion later told Ah'necca what had happened. Alouk went out on a river hunt with other warriors. Alone in his dugout canoe, he had driven his spear into a large salmon, the tether cord as usual lashed to his wrist. A seal took advantage of the restrained fish's vulnerability, grabbing it in its jaws before Alouk could haul the salmon up into his dugout. Adult harbor seals are over twice the size of a man and are extraordinarily powerful swimmers. When this one took the salmon down, Alouk's dugout canoe rolled and he was dragged out and pulled deep under the surface of the water. Alouk's companions did not see either he or the seal resurface.

Ah'necca and the tribe patrolled the riverbank for days after Alouk's disappearance. He was not ever found.

Crushed by the loss of her beloved, Ah'necca mourned incessantly until she was told that, in a dream, Elish'tie had seen Alouk's spirit with Ah'necca's—two seagulls, flying low with wings outstretched—gliding along the riverbank, into eternity together.

Ah'necca ended up living a long and useful life, in the end serving as a respected elder in the tribe. Her stories of the exploits of Alouk and his river hunter companions in action were told to the village children on school days with such vivid detail and enthusiasm that it became rare for any child of the village to ever balk at attending class.

Elish'tie remained chief of the village for the rest of her days. Never was her status challenged, as she remained loved and respected by all as a leader up until the last. As she was preparing for the passage of her spirit, she forewarned the tribe that it needed to call an assembly and determine who should be the tribe's new leader. Il'mecma, by then white-haired but still a powerful voice in the village, called for the gathering, addressed the tribe, and again provided it with an opportunity to come to a wise decision regarding her successor, even as Elish'tie's spirit was taking flight.

It was long after Elish'tie, Alouk and Ah'necca had passed, and even the spirits of their offspring were gone— at a time when the children of Po'la and Ee'na had grown up and become elders in the village—that the massive earthquake witnessed by the condor described in Chapter

Sixteen struck in the Cascadia Subduction Zone. The Pacific Ocean rose up and filled The Great River, its coastal tributaries, and the beaches and surrounding regions with flooding salt water. Massive sections of the coastal forests were inundated—many trees, even if not uprooted, gradually died simply from having been immersed in the flooding salt water—and countless plants, animals, and people in their respective habitats throughout the lowlands were totally wiped out.

But because one of its chiefs had long before had a dream, and her people had believed in her and moved their huts and possessions to a new location on high ground, the final permanent village in which Elish'tie and Alouk and Ah'necca had once lived was not destroyed by that great tsunami, nor any of those that continued to wrack the coastline, generations apart, one after another over thousands of years. Instead, the village's people were safe, and when the waters of each tsunami receded, their lives could return to normal—with each tribal generation soon able to resume their everyday business of fishing, hunting, gathering, and trading with their inland neighbors who had similarly survived the calamity of the quake and flooding waters.

Long before the white man came with horses and steel, so it was for a tribe of river hunters living on the flanks of the Great River at its confluence with the Pacific Ocean. A strong, resilient clan of hominids who fought for survival through the very dawn of humanity's emergence on the North American Continent. Early settlers of that massive

frontier, whose genetic makeup and evolved instincts, together with the subsistence methods they passed along
from generation to generation, enabled them to persist for
thousands of years in a harsh and untamed land.

RESOURCES

FOR THOSE INTERESTED IN FURTHER STUDY of humans during the Stone Age in North America, see:

"*Stone Age on the Columbia River*", by Emery Strong; Binfords & Mort, Publishers, Portland Oregon, Library of Congress Catalog Card Number: 59–14339 T–896M

"*The Eternal Frontier*", by Tim Flannery; Text Publishing, Melbourne, Australia, ISBN 0-87113-779-5

"*Guns, Germs, and Steel: The Fates of Human Societies*", by Jared Diamond; W. W. Norton & Company, ISBN 0-393-03891-2

"*The Hunt for the Lost American*" (a short story published within the book "*The Great Taos Bank Robbery and Other Indian Country Affairs*"), by Tony Hillerman; Harper Paperbacks (a division of Harper Collins), ISBN 0–06–101173–8

For a better understanding of the Cascadia Subduction Zone and Pacific Coast tsunamis, see:

William K. Thayer

"The Next Tsunami: Living on a Restless Coast", by
Bonnie Henderson; Oregon State University Press,
ISBN 978-0-087071-732-1

ABOUT THE AUTHOR

WILLIAM THAYER WAS RAISED AND EDUCATED in Oregon and California. His avocations and occupations have included being a husband, father, grandfather, lawyer, ranch hand, student, fisherman, amateur musician, literature enthusiast, and occasional writer of short pieces of fiction and nonfiction prose. He and his wife Lori live in the state of Washington.

Made in the USA
Monee, IL
28 September 2025

30599045R00083